This month, in
WORLD'S MOST ELIGIBLE TEXAN
by Sara Orwig,
meet Aaron Black—diplomat extraordinaire.
Aaron was a world-weary man-about-town who
found nothing to excite him, until...Pamela Miles
waltzed into his arms. This Plain Jane schoolteacher
was about to change his life!

**SILHOUETTE DESIRE
IS PROUD TO PRESENT THE**

Five wealthy Texas bachelors—all members of
the state's most exclusive club—set out to restore
the "Royal" jewels...and find true love.

* * *

And don't miss
LONE STAR KNIGHT
by Cindy Gerard,
next month's installment of the
Texas Cattleman's Club: Lone Star Jewels,
available only in Silhouette Desire!

Dear Reader,

Welcome to Silhouette Desire, the ultimate treat for Valentine's Day—we promise you will find six passionate, powerful and provocative romances every month! And here's what you can indulge yourself with this February....

The fabulous Peggy Moreland brings you February's MAN OF THE MONTH, *The Way to a Rancher's Heart*. You'll be enticed by this gruff widowed rancher who must let down his guard for the sake of a younger woman.

The exciting Desire miniseries TEXAS CATTLEMAN'S CLUB: LONE STAR JEWELS continues with *World's Most Eligible Texan* by Sara Orwig. A world-weary diplomat finds love—and fatherhood—after making a Plain Jane schoolteacher pregnant with his child.

Kathryn Jensen's *The American Earl* is an office romance featuring the son of a British earl who falls for his American employee. In *Overnight Cinderella* by Katherine Garbera, an ugly-duckling heroine transforms herself into a swan to win the love of an alpha male. Kate Little tells the story of a wealthy bachelor captivated by the woman he was trying to protect his younger brother from in *The Millionaire Takes a Bride*. And Kristi Gold offers *His Sheltering Arms*, in which a macho ex-cop finds love with the woman he protects.

Make this Valentine's Day extra-special by spoiling yourself with all six of these alluring Desire titles!

Enjoy!

Joan Marlow Golan

Joan Marlow Golan
Senior Editor, Silhouette Desire

Please address questions and book requests to:
Silhouette Reader Service
U.S.: 3010 Walden Ave., P.O. Box 1325, Buffalo, NY 14269
Canadian: P.O. Box 609, Fort Erie, Ont. L2A 5X3

World's Most Eligible Texan
SARA ORWIG

Silhouette®

Desire

Published by Silhouette Books
America's Publisher of Contemporary Romance

Special thanks and acknowledgment are given to
Sara Orwig for her contribution to the
TEXAS CATTLEMAN'S CLUB: LONE STAR JEWELS series.

Ladies, what fun to join the Texas Cattleman's Club with you!
Thanks to Jennifer Greene, Cindy Gerard, Kristi Gold,
Sheri WhiteFeather and our intrepid editor, Karen Kosztolnyik.

 SILHOUETTE BOOKS

ISBN 0-373-76346-8

WORLD'S MOST ELIGIBLE TEXAN

Visit Silhouette at www.eHarlequin.com

Printed in U.S.A.

Books by Sara Orwig

Silhouette Desire

Falcon's Lair #938
The Bride's Choice #1019
A Baby for Mommy #1060
Babes in Arms #1094
Her Torrid Temporary Marriage #1125
The Consummate Cowboy #1164
The Cowboy's Seductive Proposal #1192
World's Most Eligible Texan #1346

Silhouette Intimate Moments

Hide in Plain Sight #679
Galahad in Blue Jeans #971

SARA ORWIG

lives with her husband and children in Oklahoma. She has a patient husband who will take her on research trips anywhere, from big cities to old forts. She is an avid collector of Western history books. With a master's degree in English, Sara writes historical romance, mainstream fiction and contemporary romance. Books are beloved treasures that take Sara to magical worlds, and she loves both reading and writing them.

"What's Happening in Royal?"

NEWS FLASH, February—Could it possibly be true that the jaded heart of diplomat Aaron Black—most eligible of bachelors—has been softened by our local country gal Pamela Miles? The town of Royal, TX, has been a-buzzing since these two were spied dancing cheek-to-cheek during the splashy Texas Cattleman's Club gala last month...and an eyewitness saw the smitten couple dashing out the door arm-in-arm before the festivities were at an end....

In other news, Royal is still spinning from the awful emergency plane landing. No fatalities, thank our lucky stars! However, some of our Texas Cattleman's Club members have been seen rummaging through the rubble at the crash site.... What *could* they be looking for?

And two mysterious men have been noted about town, asking the whereabouts of all women who were on that flight. These ladies may be needing our cattlemen's protection—stay tuned for more!

Prologue

"**Y**ou're going home to Royal?"

"You heard me right. Can I get the family plane to pick me up?" Aaron Black persisted patiently on the phone, knowing his request was a shock to his brother.

"You're taking a leave of absence," Jeb Black repeated. "I don't believe it, but I'll have the plane there as soon as possible. The diplomat from Spain, my worldly brother, is going to take a vacation in our hometown of Royal, Texas. I'm finding this damned difficult to believe."

"The State Department has cleared it so I can take some time to go home," Aaron said. "Dammit, you take vacations."

"Yeah, with the family and we go to one of those countries you work in. We don't leave Houston to go back and sit around Royal."

"Maybe you should. Royal is nice."

"Yep, if you like cows and mesquite. I'll bet you last two

days and then you'll be calling me to send the plane to get you out of there. What about the embassy while you're gone?''

For the first time that day, Aaron was amused. He smiled in the darkness of his silent Georgetown house. ''The American Embassy in Spain can carry on nicely if the First Secretary is not there for a little while.''

''I'm not sure I'm talking to my brother. Aaron, are you all right?''

''I'm fine. Tell Mary and the boys hi for me. Better yet, give them a big hug. Thanks for sending the plane.''

''Sure. Keep in touch. And tell me one more time that you're okay.''

''I'm okay, 'Mom.'''

''Well, I'm your big brother and I have to take her place sometimes. And you'll have to admit, this isn't like you at all. Aaron—does this have something to do with the Texas Cattleman's Club?''

''Yes, it does,'' Aaron could answer honestly. His brother wasn't a member, but he could have been and he knew that the club was a facade for members to work together covertly on secret missions to save innocents' lives.

''Why didn't you tell me,'' Jeb said, sounding more relaxed. ''Take care of yourself.''

''Thanks, Jeb.'' Aaron replaced the receiver, breaking the connection with his older brother. Aaron stared out the window at the swirling snow. ''No, it isn't like me,'' he whispered to himself. ''Thanks to a tall, black-haired Texas gal, I'm doing things I've never done in my life.'' Mesmerized by the swirling snow and twinkling lights, he remembered early January, three weeks ago, the night of the Cattleman's Club gala.

Aaron's pulse accelerated as he recalled the moment he had glanced across the room and seen the willowy, black-haired woman in a simple black dress. When she'd turned, her blue-eyed gaze had met his and, just for an instant, he'd felt something spark inside him. She was laughing at something someone else had said to her. Seeing her wide blue eyes, dimples and irresistible smile, Aaron had a sudden, unreasonable compulsion to meet her. He'd thought he knew almost everyone in Royal, but she was a stranger.

Then Justin Webb had spoken to him and he'd turned to shake hands with his physician friend. The next time he'd looked back, the woman was gone from sight. It had taken him twenty more minutes to work his way through the crowd and get introduced. Another two minutes and he had her in his arms, moving on the dance floor. And then later—images taunted him of her in his arms, of the heat of her kisses, her eagerness—memories still fresh enough that his body reacted swiftly to them. Pamela Miles.

Breaking into his thoughts, a car slid to a stop before his Georgetown home and Brad Meadows, his stocky neighbor, emerged. Brad walked around the car to open the door for his wife, and then he opened the back door and leaned inside. In minutes he straightened up with his little girl in his arms. As they rushed toward their front door, they were all laughing, but then the curly-headed three-year-old looked at Aaron's house and evidently saw him standing in the window because she smiled and waved. Feeling a pang as he watched them, Aaron smiled and waved in return.

Brad Meadows had a family, a beautiful wife and a precious little girl. Aaron ran his hand across his forehead as Pamela's image floated into his thoughts again. "What the hell is the matter with me?" he mumbled. Since when did he envy a guy being *married?*

Yet he thought about his own family when he was growing up and what fun he'd had with his two brothers and sister. He glanced around his quiet living room. Empty house, empty life.

The thought nagged at him—why did he feel this way so often lately? Except that night with Pamela Miles. The loneliness, the feeling that he was missing something important in life, the hollowness he had been experiencing the last few years had vanished from the first moment he'd looked into her eyes. From that first glance the chemistry between them had been volatile. It had erupted into fiery lovemaking that at the slightest memory could make him break into a sweat. But there was something deeper than physical need. At least there had been for him.

The next morning she had been the one who'd slipped out without a word. When he'd stirred, she was gone. He had tried to shrug off the evening. When had he let a woman tie him in knots? If the lady wanted to end it that way—fine. He had to return to Washington and then to Spain and his busy life. And he knew she was going abroad to Asterland as an exchange teacher. If he wanted, he could look her up there after he was back in Spain.

He had left Royal without seeing her, flown back to D.C. and then to Spain. Two days after the ball, a private jet had left Royal, Texas, bound for Asterland with Pamela Miles on board. Not far from Royal, the plane had had to make an emergency landing. When Matt Walker, a rancher and a fellow member of the Texas Cattleman's Club, called about the landing and about other strange happenings in Royal, Aaron had tried to call Pamela, but to no avail.

The hospital had released Pamela soon after the landing and Aaron knew so little about her, he couldn't easily find her. It was clear that the lady wasn't interested in seeing him, so he tried to put her out of mind.

But Pamela Miles had a persistent way of staying in his thoughts until he was driven to constant distraction—something so foreign to his life that he decided to see her again.

As he watched snowflakes swirl and melt on the slushy narrow Georgetown street, an emptiness struck him with a chill that was far colder than the snow. He had gone into the diplomatic corps from Army intelligence, thinking he could make a difference, help change things a little in the world, but now he was losing that feeling.

Lately he had been too aware of his thirty-seven years and what little he had in his life that was really important. But the night of the Texas ball, that desolation had vanished. Pamela had brought him to life to an extent he wouldn't have guessed possible.

He swore, looking at the phone in his hand as an annoyingly loud recorded message told him his receiver was off the hook.

Aaron stared out the window, no longer seeing swirling snow or the neighboring houses with warm glows spilling from open windows. He was seeing sprawling, mesquite-covered land and a willowy, blue-eyed woman.

"Dammit," he said. "Pamela, I know there was something you felt as much as I did." He shook his head. He was being a world-class sap. The lady wasn't interested. She had made that clear. Maybe so, but he was going home to find out.

The following afternoon, the last day of January, Aaron gripped the wheel of a family car left for him at the airport as he sped down the hard-packed dusty road toward a sprawling ranch in the distance. Mesquite trees bending to the north by prevailing southern winds dotted the land on either side of the road, but all he could think about was Pamela.

He was home and he was going to find his lady.

One

"Well, I can tell you what's making you nauseated, Pamela."

She sat on the examining table with her legs crossed, the silly light cotton gown covering her as she faced white-haired Doctor Woodbury who had been treating her since she was born. She tilted her head to one side and waited, long accustomed to his blunt manner.

"You're pregnant."

"Pregnant!" Pamela's head swam and she clutched the table she was seated on with both hands. *Pregnant. It was only once. One night three weeks ago. She couldn't be.*

Dr. Woodbury was talking, but she didn't hear anything except the ringing in her ears. Her teaching job—they wouldn't want her. *Pregnant! She was going to have a baby. Baby…baby…* The word echoed in her mind. Impossible! But of course, it was possible. That night with Aaron Black. She closed her eyes and clung tightly to the cold metal, feeling as if she were going to faint.

"Knowing you as I've done through all these years, I'm guessing you'll want to keep this baby."

Dr. Woodbury's words cut through the wooziness she was experiencing. ...*keep this baby*...

She opened her eyes and placed her hand protectively against her stomach. "Yes! Of course, I'll keep my baby," she snapped, her head clearing swiftly. How could he think she wouldn't!

His blue eyes gazed undisturbed at her as he shrugged stooped shoulders. "After she had you, your mother had two abortions. She wasn't having any more babies."

"I'm not my mother," Pamela said stiffly, suddenly seeing how not only Dr. Woodbury, but everyone else in town would see her—with morals as loose as her mother's had been. The town tramp. That was what Dolly Miles had been called too many times. Pamela remembered the teasing, the whispers, and worse, the steady stream of men who came and went through the Miles's tiny house.

She was shocked to learn there had been two abortions. When she thought about it, though, she wasn't surprised. Dolly thought of no one except herself. Two abortions. Pamela had a strange sense of loss. She might have had brothers or sisters. She pressed her hand against her stomach as she tried to focus on what Dr. Woodbury was saying.

"I'm keeping my baby."

"I thought you would," he said complacently. "You seem in perfectly good health. I'm going to put you on some vitamins, and then you make an appointment to come back this time next month."

The rest of the hour she moved in a daze that lasted through running errands, getting her vitamins and heading to the Royal Diner to eat. It was early for lunch and the diner would be empty, which suited her fine. Right now she didn't feel like seeing anyone. Thank heavens Aaron Black had gone back to Spain. She would have three or four months before her pregnancy would show, so she would have to make her plans in that time.

The brisk wind was chilly, catching the door to the diner and fluttering the muslin curtains at the windows, following her into the diner in a gust that swirled dried leaves around her feet. The little brass bell over the door tinkled. She glanced at the long, Formica counter top, the red vinyl-covered barstools and headed toward an empty booth along the wall. The jukebox was quiet. She put her head in her hands, her elbows propped on the table, while she thought about her pregnancy.

"Hi, Pamela," came a sharp voice, and she looked up at Sheila Foster, who plopped a plastic-coated menu into her hands. The Royal Diner—Food Fit For A King! was lettered across the top. Trying to focus on the words, Pamela skimmed the menu and ordered one of Manny's delicious hamburgers and a chocolate malt, knowing she would have to start thinking in terms of healthy meals because of the baby. The baby. She was going to have a baby. She was pregnant!

She couldn't believe the news. First sheer terror had gripped her because she didn't know how to be a mother and being unwed and pregnant was still scandalous in Royal, Texas. But the terror was quickly replaced with awe. And then when Dr. Woodbury had asked her if she would keep her baby, reality had come and she'd known she wanted her baby with every fiber in her body.

A precious baby all her own. She had never once expected to have her own baby. She had rarely dated. What Aaron had found in her, even for one night, she couldn't imagine. Except she had easily fallen into his arms, succumbed to his charms, returned his lovemaking with unbridled passion.

As she sat waiting for her lunch, her mind went back to that magical night of the Texas Cattleman's Club gala.

The gala had been given to celebrate the European dignitaries who were visiting Royal from Asterland and Obersbourg and to thank the members of the local Texas Cattleman's Club for their help in the rescue of Princess Anna von Oberland, now married to Greg Hunt. It was a glittering array of diplomats and titled people including Asterland's Lady Helena

Reichard. It had been a cold, clear night, and when Pamela
had walked into the light and warmth of the ballroom, she had
wondered what she was doing there. Yet, it had sounded like
fun when Thad Delner, her recently widowed principal, had
told her he had to make an appearance and would she like to
go, since his invitation included a guest.

While Thad had talked to friends and she had talked to
people she knew, they'd drifted apart. As she stood in a circle
of acquaintances, she felt compelled to turn. Glancing across
the room, she looked into the green-eyed gaze of a tall, ruggedly handsome man. Looking dashing in his black tux and
white shirt, he had stared at her too intently, a little too long
to be a casual glance. Broad-shouldered yet lean, he had short,
neatly combed dark brown hair. His features were rugged with
a prominent bone structure, but it was his thickly lashed green
eyes that mesmerized and held her.

As she gazed back at him, time was suspended. Her pulse
jumped: it was as if he had reached across the room and
touched her.

Then Justin Webb had spoken to him, and he'd turned away
to talk to his friend.

She knew who he was. Aaron Black. Older, an American
diplomat stationed abroad, he was from Royal. Everyone in
town knew the Black family. Old money, but down-to-earth
good people.

Trying to concentrate and forget the look from the disturbing stranger, she turned back to the conversation at hand.

And then she was looking into his eyes only a few feet from
her as he extended his hand. "Fun party. I'm Aaron Black."
His voice was low, husky and mellow. She'd placed her hand
in his and his grip was solid, his fingers warm, curling around
hers.

"I'm Pamela Miles."

"Native?"

"Yes," she'd answered, wondering how he could possibly
not know. She'd thought everyone in town knew Dolly Miles,
and that Dolly had a daughter.

"I haven't spotted your date hovering over you."

She'd laughed. "You won't. I'm here with Thad Delner, my principal. I teach second grade at Royal Elementary, and Thad has been recently widowed. He had an invitation for tonight, and thought he needed to attend briefly to represent Royal Elementary, so he asked if I would like to come along. I've never been to one of these balls before."

"Well, since no date will be breathing down my neck—want to dance?"

When she'd nodded, he'd taken her arm to steer her to the dance floor and then she was closer than ever to him, aware of the cottony scent of his stiffly starched shirt, his cologne. Her fingers brushed his neck as she put her arm on his shoulder to dance. His hand holding hers was warm. They moved together as if they had danced with each other forever.

His cheekbones were prominent and his lower lip full, sensual. She realized she was staring at his mouth, and her gaze flew back up to meet his. She saw fires in the depth of his emerald eyes. Once again her gaze was caught and held by his and conversation fled while her heart drummed. As the moment stretched, making her breathless, tension crackled between them. With an effort of will she looked away.

"Tell me about your life, Pamela," he said. "You're here with your principal. Does this mean there's no guy in your life right now?"

"Yes, it does. I lead an ordinary teacher's life except I'm going to Asterland in two days as an exchange teacher."

"You're the one!" Aaron's eyebrow arched, and he tilted his head as he leaned away slightly to study her. "This is my lucky day. I'm with the American Embassy in Spain. On weekends we can see each other," he said with a warmth in his voice that sent a tingle through her. "Lucky Asterland. It's a pretty place. Very different from West Texas," he drawled.

She laughed. "I'd imagined that."

She'd listened to him talk as they danced through two more dances, and then his arm had tightened and they were dancing cheek-to-cheek and her pulse was racing.

She'd danced once with Matt Walker, an old friend and one of the local ranchers, and then Aaron was back, claiming her for another dance. And she was aware of other women watching Aaron, and she knew they wanted to be dancing with him, and she could understand why they did. As they'd spun around the floor to a fast number, she looked at women in fancy gowns they had bought for thousands of dollars in elegant boutiques here in Royal or in stores in Dallas and Houston while she was in her simple black sheath she had purchased for a little over fifty dollars. She was amazed that Aaron was dancing with her—amazed and glad. And in some ways, it seemed the most natural thing in the world to be in his arms, moving with him, looking into his green eyes.

After an hour, between dances, Thad Delner had joined them. As soon as she introduced him to Aaron, Thad had turned to her to tell her he was ready to leave. Before he could finish, Aaron broke in.

"I'll take Pamela home, Mr. Delner. I'm glad you brought her."

Thad Delner's blue eyes focused on her with a questioning look. "Is that all right with you, Pamela?"

She'd nodded, breathless, amazed Aaron was offering to take her home "Yes, it's fine," she said, looking at Aaron, whose rugged handsomeness made her heart race.

"All right. You two go back to your dancing. I'll talk to you before you leave for Asterland, Pamela."

"Thanks for bringing me, Thad," she'd said and then she was back in Aaron's arms to dance again.

When he'd invited her to come by his house for a drink, and she'd accepted, the dreamlike quality of the evening continued. At Pine Valley, an exclusive area of fine homes, Aaron slowed for large iron gates to open. As a gate swung back, he drove past it and waved at the guard.

The stately mansions sobered her. The lawns were vast and well-cared-for, the houses imposing, and his world of wealth and privilege seemed light years from her world of teaching and budgeting and ordinary living.

"Why so quiet?" Aaron asked. The lights of the dash threw the flat planes of his cheeks into shadow. When he looked at her, she could feel his probing look. Handsome, dashing, he was incredibly unique.

"I was just thinking about the differences in our lives," she said, looking at the palatial Georgian-style houses with sweeping, constantly tended lawns. "We're very different, you and I," she said solemnly.

"Thank heavens," he said lightly and picked up her hand to brush her knuckles across his cheek. "If you were just like me, I wouldn't be taking you home with me now, I can promise."

She smiled at him and relaxed, but the feeling returned again when they entered his house and he turned off an alarm.

"Gates, guards and alarms. You're well-protected."

He shrugged. "This is a family home. Ninety percent of the time, no one lives here," he said, taking her arm as he switched on a low light in the entryway.

"I'm sorry you lost your parents," she said, remembering headlines several years ago that had told about the plane crash in Denmark when his parents and six other Texans had been killed.

"Thanks. What about your parents?"

"They're deceased," she said stiffly, amazed again that he didn't know about her mother. She had never known her father and wasn't certain her mother even knew which man fathered her.

Aaron had led her through a kitchen and down a wide hall into a large family room elegantly furnished with plush navy leather and deeply burnished cherrywood furniture. An immense redbrick fireplace was at one end of the room and a thick Oriental rug covered part of the polished oak floor. He crossed the room to the fireplace to start the fire and in minutes the logs blazed. Following him into the room, she wandered around to look at oil paintings of western scenes. When she glanced back at him, he'd shed his tux coat. As her gaze ran across his broad shoulders, she drew a deep breath. He removed his tie and unfastened his collar and there was something so personal in watching him shed part of his clothing, that her cheeks flushed.

As soon as he moved to the bar, he glanced at her. "Wine, beer, whiskey, soda pop, what would you like to drink?"

"White wine sounds fine," she answered, watching his well-shaped hands move over sparkling crystal while she sat on a corner of the cool leather sofa. He joined her, handing her a glass. When he sat down, he raised his glass. "Here's to tonight, the night we met, Pamela," he said softly and his words were like a caress.

While she smiled at him, she touched her glass lightly to his. "You think tonight is going to be memorable? You're a sweet-talkin' devil, Aaron Black. You're dangerous," she said, flirting with him and watching his green eyes sparkle. Yet even as she teased him, she had a feeling that his words, *tonight, the night we met,* would stick with her forever.

"I'm dangerous? I think that's good news," he said, sipping his wine and setting it on the large glass and cherrywood table in front of them. He scooted closer to her and reached out, picking up locks of her hair and letting them slide through his fingers. She was too aware of his faint touches, his knuckles just barely brushing her throat and ear and cheek. "Now why am I dangerous?"

"All that fancy talking can turn a girl's head mighty fast. Texas men are too good at it."

"And Texas women are the prettiest women in the world," he said softly, his gaze running over her features.

She laughed and set her wine on the table as she looked at him with amusement. His brows arched in question. "That is high-fallutin' talkin'! I'm too tall, too freckled and there's never been a time in my entire life that anyone told me what a beauty I am, so that's a stretch, Aaron."

He didn't smile in return which made her heart miss a beat, but he gazed at her solemnly while he stroked his fingers through her hair. "Maybe I see something others haven't seen."

"Oh, heavens, can you lay it on thick!"

"Just telling the truth," he drawled and smiled a lazy smile at her.

They were in dangerous waters and she glanced around, trying to get the conversation less personal. "If no one lives here most of the time, who takes care of your house?" she asked, looking at the immaculate room.

"We have a staff," he answered casually without taking his eyes from hers. His fingers stroked her nape in featherlight brushes that ignited fires deep within her. His voice was low. The only light now was from the blazing fire, and there was a cozy intimacy that was made electric by his nearness. "Why are you a teacher?"

"I love children," she answered, and he nodded his approval. "I feel strongly that all children should be able to read, so I like working with them, particularly in reading. I never had any family. Maybe that's why I feel the way I do about kids. Why did you want to be a diplomat?"

"Everything about it fascinated me," he said quietly, his green gaze studying her as if he were memorizing every feature. "I thought I could help save the world when I went into it."

"And now?"

"Now I know that's an impossibility. The old world will keep turning no matter what I do. There will always be wars and intrigue, and now, more than ever, terrorism."

"You sound disenchanted."

"Not tonight. Tonight is good," he said, giving her a heated, direct look that blatantly conveyed his desire.

"Behave yourself, Aaron! You do come on strong."

"You won't believe me, but I don't usually." As she smiled, he touched her cheek. "Dimples. You have to have been told your dimples are pretty."

"Maybe so," she said. "Tell me about Spain."

"I'll tell you, but soon I want to show it to you. You'll have your weekends free when you get to Asterland and I can take you to my favorite places in Spain."

Though she merely smiled at him, his words gave her a thrill. She listened to him describe Spain and Asterland, and she answered his questions about her job. Their conversation roamed over a myriad of subjects as if they had a million things to tell each other. And all the time they talked, his fingers drifted over her hands or nape or ear or played in her hair while he watched her as if she were the first woman he had ever seen.

"Your family has lived in Texas for more than a hundred years, haven't they?" she asked him. He nodded while his fingers stroked her nape and she barely could concentrate on what he was answering. While his index finger traced the curve of her ear, she inhaled deeply, tingles fueling her desire.

"Yep. My great-granddaddy, Pappy Black, ran cattle when he came home after the War Between the States. He amassed the Black fortune. Then my granddad, Rainy Black—I'm named for him—he was Aaron Rainier Black, was a Texas senator, so I grew up around politicians. I'm as Texas as you can get."

"Sure, Aaron," she said, thinking of his eastern education. His fingers trailed from her ear down over her throat and along her arm, moving to her knee. His thickly lashed eyes were filled with desire and she tingled along every nerve ending from all his feather touches. "*¿Habla Español?*" she asked.

"*Sí. ¿Y usted?*"

"*Muy poco.* Only what I've picked up from living in Royal. What other languages do you speak?"

"French, German, Arabic, Italian, Polish and Chinese. My undergraduate degree is in languages and political science and I had to learn Arabic in the military. I had to learn Polish with the State Department."

She thought again of the vast differences in their lives. "Which colleges did you attend?"

"Harvard for an undergraduate degree," he replied in an offhand manner. "Now tell me what you like to do? What's fun?"

"Playing with little children, reading. I enjoy doing pencil drawings. Just simple things. I've taught aerobics before, but not for the past year.'' Her gaze dropped to his mouth, and she wondered what it would be like to kiss him. She wanted to kiss him. Why did he have this effect on her? She felt as if sparks constantly danced between them, and her awareness level was at a maximum. With an effort she tried to concentrate on what he was saying.

They sat and talked until a grandfather clock in the hall chimed three in the morning. It seemed she had been with him five minutes, yet it seemed as if she had known him all her life.

By three he had unfastened and removed his cuff links, turned back his white sleeves, kicked off his shoes. Her nerves were tingling and raw, and she was intensely aware of him, looking at his full lower lip and continuing to wonder what it would be like to kiss him.

When the clock softly chimed the third time, she stood. ''Well, it's getting late,'' she said.

In a fluid movement, he came to his feet instantly and placed his hand on her waist, turning her to face him. One look in his eyes and her breath caught. He drew her closer.

''I feel like I've waited all my life for this moment,'' he said softly.

Her heart thudded, and she told herself not to believe what he said, but the words thrilled her as his hand slid behind her head and his arm went around her waist, pulling her against his hard length. He leaned down, his mouth brushing hers and her pulse skipped with the first contact of his lips on hers. Fire and magic. Even more, before her lashes came down, was the look in his eyes of wanting her—as if his words had been the truth and he had been waiting forever.

What was it about this man that melted her physically and emotionally? That made all barriers go down and her body and heart both yield completely? He took her breath and made her pulse race and it seemed so incredibly right, as if she were destined for this night from the day she was born. He rubbed his lips softly against hers again.

"Aaron," she whispered his name, that from the first moment they'd met had been special, irresistible.

His mouth settled on hers, opening it fully while his tongue thrust over hers, stroking it and conveying such need that she quivered in response. She wrapped her arms around his neck and returned his kisses and his passion. She felt his arousal and felt his hands slide over her and then move to her zipper. Cool air played across her shoulders as her dress fell away, and Aaron raised his head to push away the top of her lacy blue teddy. Inhaling deeply, he cupped her small breasts in his large, tanned hands. His breathing was ragged when he bent, and his tongue stroked her nipple.

"You're beautiful," he whispered. "I need you."

His words were as seductive as his kisses. Moaning with pleasure, she shook and gripped his shoulders and knew she should stop, but his every touch was magic. Sensations and desire bombarded her. Never in her life had she known passion. Never before had she found a man who ignited desire into blazing flames. She would stop him, but oh, not yet. Not yet...

His thumbs circled and stroked her taut nipples and her insides turned a somersault. Her fingers went to the studs on his shirt, and in minutes she had worked them free and pushed away his shirt and then her hands were on his chest that was lean, hard-corded muscles. Her fingers tangled in the mat of short brown hair across his chest.

Swinging her into his arms while he kissed her, he carried her to a bedroom and then they were in bed together, her length stretched against his. As he peeled away the teddy and her hose, his hands and kisses were everywhere.

Was it the wine? The man? The magic of the night? His beguiling words that made her feel an incredible need in him for her alone?

A dim voice within her urged her usual caution, but it went up in smoke in minutes as he moved lower, trailing kisses to her thighs. His hand slipped between her legs, stroking her, driving her over a brink and making her want what she had never known, want it all with this man who was so special to her from the first moment she had looked into his eyes.

She helped him peel away his trousers and briefs. He moved over her, hard, ready, breathtakingly handsome as she wrapped her long legs around him and pulled him to her. She heard him whisper, asking if she was protected, and she answered yes, yes, wanting him with a desperate urgency in a manner she hadn't ever dreamed possible while desire demolished all her wisdom and caution.

His mouth covered hers, taking her cries of passion as he slowly entered her. When he raised his head and frowned, she arched her hips, tightened her legs, and pulled him to her.

"Please, Aaron," she whispered, knowing this night was more than magic for her and she wanted him as she had never wanted anything. She gave her virginity to him eagerly, wanting him and lost in the roaring of her pulse, only dimly hearing him cry out her name as she gasped, carried out of the world into pure ecstasy, finally tumbling over a brink of release.

In the quiet of the fading night he showered her with kisses, and then he held her tightly against him while they talked. His other hand caressed her, and his voice was a deep rumble that she loved to listen to.

"What do you like best in the world, Aaron?" she asked, wanting to discover everything about him she could.

"This night. You in my arms. Long, slow hot kisses, people who care, Switzerland, the ranch. What do you like?" he asked in a lazy voice while he languidly drew his fingers over her hip.

"Tonight, too. Being with you. Little children. Books." She ran her finger along his jaw that had a faint trace of stubble now. "What do you want out of life?"

"Ahh, that's an easier question. I want a family, a woman who is my best friend and lover. I want to do some good for people, to settle on the ranch—"

"You want to live here on your ranch?" she asked, interrupting him and surprised by his answer.

"Sure. I grew up on the ranch and love it. I want some

more years in the diplomatic service, but then I want to come home to ranching. What do you want out of life?'' he asked, gazing into her eyes while she caught his hand to kiss his knuckles lightly.

''I don't think about it much. I want to be a good teacher. I don't want any child to ever pass through my classroom and not be able to read when moving on. They should all learn in first and second grade and never go on until they master reading.''

''No yearning for marriage?''

She was glad it was dark and he couldn't see her blush, because she could feel the heat rise in her cheeks. ''You know now, Aaron, that you're the first man in my life. I've never dated much and never thought I would marry.''

''I'll bet the ranch you do.''

When she laughed, he touched her dimple. ''Are you a gambling man?''

''Actually no. But I don't think that would be much of a bet. You'll marry, lady.''

''Right now, I'm thinking about going to Asterland. Tell me some more about Europe.''

''Asterland is a beautiful little country. You're going to like it.'' She listened to him talk for another twenty minutes and then while she was talking, she heard his deep, regular breathing and realized he was asleep. Hugging him, knowing she would carry memories of this night with her the rest of her life because she had fallen in love, she settled against him and closed her eyes.

She lay in his arms and listened to his heartbeat and his deep steady breathing. He held her tightly as if afraid of losing her. The wonder of the night left her dazed. Aaron was a marvel. Their lovemaking was ecstasy she had never expected to experience. She'd slept, then stirred as dawn spilled into the room, and along with it, reality.

Memories assailed her, and in the light of day, they held clarity and a shocked realization of how he must see the night. How could she have fallen into his arms and given all to him the first night she'd met him? She closed her eyes in pain, thinking of her mother and the taunting cries she had been teased with when she was young—"…your mom's the town tramp," "trash mama," "she's cheap," "easy lay"—even worse names.

Shame, shock, fear of what Aaron would think of her, all ran through her mind. Was she that much like her mother after all? After all these years of being so circumspect, so careful, the moment a dashing, worldly man had turned his charm on her, she had thrown prudence over instantly.

Wiping at tears that stung her eyes, she slid out of bed. She could only imagine how Aaron must see her. Then her gaze fell on him and, momentarily, her feelings shifted and longing shook her. He was sprawled in bed, the sheet down below his narrow waist. His body was lean, muscled and looked like the body of a runner. The mat of dark brown hair across his chest tapered down in a line to his navel. Her gaze traveled lower to the sheet covering him, but her memories conjured up visions of Aaron last night when he was hard, ready and so incredibly male and appealing.

Giving a little shake of her shoulders, she knew she didn't want to see those probing green eyes open and look at her in a demeaning manner. Nor did she want to hear him make excuses or make light of an evening that had taken her heart. Again, she wondered how she could have succumbed so swiftly. Was it in her genes? She had fought that notion all her life, treating boys coldly, keeping barriers around her when she was older, barriers that turned guys off quickly.

As quietly as possible, with shaking hands and tears stinging her eyes, she gathered her things and dressed. Then she slipped downstairs and called Royal's only cab.

In minutes she was standing on the drive, praying that Aaron wouldn't waken. Today she was supposed to go to Midland to see her closest friend, Jessica Atkins, a fellow teacher. Aaron probably couldn't find her if he wanted to. She suspected he wouldn't even care. Yet he hadn't seemed that way last night.

"Of course, he didn't, ninny!" she whispered to herself. "Get real. He seduced you—it was a one-night stand and you fell into his arms eagerly. Practically jumped into his arms."

The cab whisked her away, and when the tall iron gates began to swing shut behind her she was certain she was closing a part of her life away. From this time forward, last night would only be a memory, yet she knew she had given Aaron much more than just her body.

Embarrassed and saddened, she had ridden home, packed for the weekend swiftly and rushed to her car to drive to Midland and the haven of Jessica's small frame house. No matter how many miles she put between them, she couldn't get Aaron out of her thoughts. The realization that they hadn't used any protection came to her. Aaron had asked if she was protected, and, totally lost to the moment, wanting him as she had never wanted anything in her life, she had whispered yes.

"You know better than that!" she said aloud to herself.

Realizing she was sitting in the Royal Diner, talking to herself, Pamela took a deep breath. Aaron had asked if she was protected. She couldn't blame him. And if he learned about her pregnancy—that must never happen. She wouldn't even consider the possibilities.

She thought about the Blacks. Everyone in town knew that his parents had been into missionary work; his brother was a minister, channeling funds to worldwide missions, his older sister was a doctor in a third-world country. She didn't know what his other brother did, but they were good people and used their enormous wealth to help others. Aaron had told her how he had gone into the diplomatic service because he thought he could try to do something to help world situations.

She ran her fingers across her brow. Aaron Black must never know he was the father of her baby. He would be a man to marry out of a sense of duty and doing the right thing. Aaron...

Such a pang hit her she clutched her middle. Longing rolled up through her like a tidal wave. Along with her body, she had given her heart to him. She knew that. But she was realistic. She was a veteran of watching pillars of the community sleep with her mother, give Dolly tokens of appreciation—or much more than tokens—cars, jewelry, but always they eventually turned their backs on Dolly and went their own way. And out in public she had seen them meet her mother and seen the furtive glances, the coolness, the lack of respect they had treated Dolly with.

She couldn't bear that with Aaron. Aaron Black's baby. Again, she pressed her hand to her flat stomach and felt a surge of maternal joy. She already loved this baby with her whole heart and she would devote her life to her precious child.

She would have to move from Royal because there would be too much gossip here, but that was something she didn't have to worry about today. She just had to keep her condition a secret until her plans were made. It was a secret to be kept most of all from Aaron Black. He had already gone back to Europe, so there was little chance of his finding out unless Justin Webb or Matt Walker or another one of those buddies of Aaron's learned about it and told him. And if he did find out, Matt was a good enough friend to respect her wishes. She could trust Matt to be the friend he always had been.

Once again the enormity of what she had done struck her. How could she have been so like her mother? How could she have thrown over all her caution when she had spent a lifetime being cautious? The man could charm the proverbial birds out of the trees, but that was no excuse. She had met charmers in college and had managed easily to say no. What was it about Aaron Black that twisted her into knots, melted her reserve, dissolved all barriers she kept up?

She clutched her middle again, aghast when she thought about how easy she had been, how careless, and what Aaron must think about her.

"Are you feeling better, Pamela?"

"I'm fine, thanks," she said, aware of the waitress ap

proaching the table. Sheila's pink uniform was bright and her gaze was sharp.

"What happened was scary. I guess you'll get over it as time goes by. Sorry you won't get to go to Asterland to teach this semester. I heard the program was suspended."

"That's right, but with my ankle hurt, I wasn't able to teach right after the crash," Pamela said, wishing they could stop talking about it.

Sheila turned away, and Pamela stared at the giant burger and golden fries on her plate and knew she couldn't eat a bite. Nor could she leave the entire burger and fries without stirring up a storm of comments. She sipped some of the chocolate malt, ate two bites of the burger, and then she couldn't get down another morsel. She wrapped the burger and a few fries in her napkin and jammed them into her purse. Her purse would reek of hamburger, but she didn't want any gossip starting now. No one ordered one of Manny's juicy burgers and then left it with only a couple of bites taken out of it.

Thank heavens, so far, both she and Thad Delner led such straight and square lives that no one could conjure up gossip about them going together to the ball. And everyone in town knew he went to represent the school. Also, everyone in town was sorry about the loss of his wife, whom he had deeply loved. But once word got out that she had left the ball with Aaron Black, that would be another matter.

She slid out of the booth, paid and rushed from the diner before she had another conversation with anyone else. A few people were beginning to appear for lunch and she greeted them perfunctorily without even seeing who they were.

She drove home, her thoughts still churning, but an absolute determination growing within her that Aaron Black should never know about the baby. Their baby. She would call Jessica to tell her to watch for teaching jobs in Midland. The teaching position in Asterland was suspended this semester and by the next term, she would be very pregnant and she wouldn't want to go to Asterland even if it were possible. She wanted her baby born here in Texas where she had friends.

Midland was larger than Royal, far enough away that her life would be her own, yet close enough she could get back to see her friends in Royal when she wanted to.

At least she didn't have to worry about running into Aaron. He was halfway around the world and most likely had forgotten about her by now. She could imagine the kind of women in his life and wondered whether, while home in Texas, he had simply been amusing himself with the country girl that she was. In many ways Royal wasn't a typical small Texas town because of oil money and all the wealth it produced. Basically, though, Royal *was* a small West Texas town and she was pure country.

She turned onto her street and saw her two-story brick apartment complex. She drove through the open wooden barrier that never closed and turned down the row to the back of her tiny apartment and her carport. As she approached her carport her heart thudded. Seated on the tailgate of a shiny black pickup was Aaron Black.

Two

Her throat went dry and it was difficult to breathe. She felt hot, embarrassed, as if she were nine months pregnant instead of only weeks. There he was, and more than that, he looked marvelous. Her pulse raced like a shooting star. He looked as good in jeans and a plaid woolen shirt as he had in a tux. He wore scuffed boots and slid casually to his feet with his hands hooked into his wide, hand-tooled leather belt. A lock of brown hair fell across his forehead.

His green eyes were just as she remembered—going right through her. How could she keep her secret? *Why was he here and not halfway around the world?* What was she going to say to him? What did he want?

A cynical voice answered *that* question in a flash—another easy night with her. Her chin raised and her lips compressed while she tried to breathe deeply and wondered if she was going to faint right in front of him. Except she wasn't given to fainting. It might be a lot easier if she could.

"Go away, Aaron Black," she mumbled as she parked, and

knew he was watching her every move. And then he was at the door, opening it and holding it for her.

When she stepped outside and looked up at him, her heart skipped beats. Gazing at him solemnly, she wrestled with her feelings because she wanted to walk right into his arms.

"Hi, Pamela."

She couldn't say a word.

"Well, hi, there, Aaron, it's good to see you," he said in a teasing voice while he ran his finger lightly along her cheek. "Cat got your tongue? Some reason I developed the plague and you want to avoid me?"

At his touch, tingles flashed through her, and she knew she was hopelessly lost unless she got her wits together and her defenses up. She drew herself up. "Hi, Aaron. I thought you were in Spain."

"Well, I was," he drawled in that mellow voice that was like a stroke of his fingers. Darn, if he would just quit looking at her like she was a bit of steak and he was a starving man. "But I came home because I wanted to see you."

"You came home to see me?" she whispered, shocked and unable to believe she had heard correctly. Did he *know?* She rejected that notion instantly.

He looked around while a gust of cold wind buffeted them and spun leaves into the air. "Could we maybe talk inside?"

"Oh! Of course. Come in," she said, feeling ridiculous and knowing the women in his life knew how to handle moments like this smoothly and casually, while she was acting like a twelve-year-old with her first crush. She moved ahead of him, reached out to unlock the door and dropped her keys. He scooped them up, reached his long arm around her and unlocked the door, pushing it open and waiting for her to enter. Too aware of how close he was behind her, she stepped inside. He made her fluttery and overly conscious of him and of herself and her condition.

She glanced around her tiny kitchen and thought of his palatial family home in Pine Valley. Her whole apartment would fit into his kitchen.

She opened her purse to drop her keys inside and the smell of the hamburger wafted into the air. His brows arched and he reached down to pull the wrapped burger from her purse. She could hear the laughter in his voice. "You carry hamburgers and fries in your purse?"

"Not usually," she said, snatching her lunch from him and carrying it to the counter to set it down. "I wasn't hungry. Do you want anything to drink?"

"No thanks, but help yourself."

She shook her head. "Let's sit in the living room."

He looked all around as they entered her tiny living room with its white wicker furniture, red, blue and yellow throw pillows, colorful prints on the walls—an attractive room to her, but a far cry from his lifestyle.

"Nice place."

"Thank you."

He prowled around with both the grace and curiosity of a cat and stepped into the bedroom that opened off the living room. "This is your bedroom," he said, and she wondered how she had left her room that morning when she had dressed for the doctor's appointment. She ran her hand across her forehead, watching him as he returned to the living room and moved across the room to the sofa. He tilted his head again.

"Are you going to sit down?"

"Yes," she replied, knowing she was acting ridiculously, but he had jolted her with his sudden appearance when she'd thought he was in Spain.

When she perched on the edge of the sofa, he sank down near her, looking relaxed and as if he owned the place. He leaned closer, and she realized she should have sat across the room from him. He ran his finger along her cheek. "Big blue eyes just like I remembered," he said softly, and she wondered if he could hear her heart thudding.

"Why are you here?"

Again, he looked as if amusement danced in his eyes. "Glad to see me?"

"Yes," she said cautiously. This time there was no mistaking the laughter in his eyes.

"Uh-huh," he drawled. "Can I ask you a question?"

"Sure," she said, bracing up and wondering what was coming.

"Why did you disappear the next morning?" His voice was quiet, his words innocuous, but his eyes nailed her and a flush heated her cheeks.

With an effort she looked away from those damnable green eyes that made her feel as if he could see every thought in her head. "I was supposed to leave town and I needed to get home."

"Oh, yeah," he drawled in a voice that indicated he didn't believe that answer for a second.

She knotted her fingers in her lap. "I don't usually sleep with a guy the first night I meet him," she whispered stiffly, feeling her cheeks burn, but there it was, the flat-out bald truth.

"I know you don't," he said in such a tender voice that she wanted to fling herself into his arms. His fingers lifted her chin and turned her to face him, and when she looked into his eyes, she felt she was melting and all her resistance was slipping away.

"Go to dinner with me tonight."

"I can't be—"

"That's why I came home," he interrupted.

Shocked by his statement, she stared at him. "It isn't either! You didn't come home to take me to dinner."

"Did so," he argued quietly. "To my way of thinking, we have some unfinished business between us," he said, and beneath his soft voice, she could hear a steely determination.

She thought about her condition and shook her head. "I think it is finished," she said. "You move in one world and I live in another. I'm just a country girl, Aaron, so let's be realistic. You couldn't have come home to take me to dinner!"

"Yes, ma'am, I surely did," slipping into a West Texas drawl that she knew he didn't usually have. "And what's all this about a country girl? Where do you think I grew up?"

"Right here, but don't give me that ol' country-boy routine. You were educated in the east and you live abroad and you move in circles that I know nothing about and the women in your life—"

"Bore me witless," he said, scooting a little closer. "I wouldn't pursue this if I didn't feel like there was something between us."

His words devastated her, and she clutched her fingers even more tightly together. *Resist the sweet talk, resist...*

She scooted away from him a few inches, keeping the space they'd had, but now she was pressed against the end of the sofa.

"We had sex between us, but—"

"That was lovemaking, Pamela," he interrupted with such solemnity that her heart did another lurch. "It was good and fine and important." He studied her. "Maybe we need to take some time now to get to know each other."

"No, we don't!"

"Why the hell not?"

Her mind raced on how to answer him. *Why did he have to sit so close?* It was difficult to think. "I told you, I'm country and you're not and don't say you are. Our worlds are really different, and there is no way you can convince me that you're here because I'm so fascinating."

"You don't think so?"

"No. How'd did you get off work in the middle of the week?"

"I asked for time off to come home to see you."

Her jaw did drop. While she stared at him, he gazed back steadily with no amusement in his features now.

"This is important," he announced solemnly.

Her heart stopped. Missed beats and then picked up. *No. Not now,* was all she could think. *Not now. Don't do this. He mustn't know.* Her head swam. *This can't happen now. It's too late. Much too late for us.*

She shook her head. "You need to pack and go back to Spain. This is ridiculous. We're in different worlds, Aaron.

That night was special, but it was just a night. Now I need to—''

He moved closer. ''Pamela, I want a chance to show you that our worlds aren't that different. There are some basic things about people that match up, and I think we ought to get to know each other a little and see how much we match up. Maybe you're right and it won't be the magic it seemed, but let's get to know each other a little better and give a relationship a chance.''

''I just don't think we should.'' She could barely get out the words.

''What will it hurt?'' he persisted softly, lacing his fingers in hers and running his thumb across her knuckles and scrambling her thoughts.

If you only knew, you would run like crazy. She stared at him, her heart pounding, knowing that she had to send him on his way.

''You're sitting close.''

''I'm glad you noticed. What will it hurt?''

I will be in love with you more than I am now, she thought, *and you'll find out I'm carrying your baby, and then you'll want to marry me for all the wrong reasons.* She knew she could never, ever let him know about the pregnancy. Send him on his way back to Spain.

''One little dinner date,'' he said softly, leaning forward to brush his lips against her throat. ''Just go out with me tonight, okay? Come on. I'll bet we'll have a good time getting to know each other a little better,'' he coaxed. He was close enough that she could feel his warmth, smell his woodsy aftershave.

''We shouldn't—''

''You'd rather eat alone than with me?'' he whispered.

''No, but—''

''Good. It's settled.'' His lips trailed kisses lightly along her throat, and she ached to turn her head and kiss him fully. With that first brush of his lips, she was lost. He leaned back. ''I'll pick you up about seven. I made reservations at Claire's.''

Her eyes opened. What had she done? How did he get his way so easily with her?

"Aaron, you couldn't have come back from Spain to take me to dinner."

"Yes, I did."

If he was lying, he was doing a magnificent job of sounding convincing, but then she knew in his job he must be accustomed to some slick talking to get what he wanted.

"But what about your job? You can't just leave on a whim."

"I have so many vacation days piled up, I can take off for a long time. When I started this job, I was in love with it. I guess I thought I was doing my part to help save the world. I gave it my everything. I didn't take vacations very often, so I have a lot of days coming. Besides, I asked for a leave of absence and they granted it."

Appalled, she stared at him. "Leave of absence! You're in Royal for more than tonight?"

"Don't sound so thrilled," he drawled, and his eyes were full of questions. "You keep looking at me as if I'm some kind of monster."

"No! Oh, no! I just am shocked about your leave of absence. It takes some adjusting to think of you in Royal instead of Spain."

He placed both hands on either side of her face while his gaze probed hers. "Why does it take some adjusting to have me here? That's not too flattering."

"I'm sorry," she said, heat burning her cheeks. Why couldn't she control her darn blushes! "I'm just surprised."

"Well, get used to it, lady, because I came home for us to get to know each other a little better," he said in a husky voice.

She pulled away from him and stood, her knees bumping his knees. He was on his feet instantly and his hand rested on her waist, stopping her from moving away from him.

"Pamela, I don't know what's going on in that pretty head

of yours, but yes, I want us to get to know each other better. I've been thinking about you constantly since that night.''

"Oh, my heavens! I don't believe it.''

He frowned. "Well, you better believe it, and I'll do my damnedest to convince you because memories of you have played hell with my work. You've got some notion in your head about the kind of woman I want in my life, but you're wrong.''

"Oh, Aaron,'' she said, his words tearing at her.

"At least, let's just take a little time. Maybe we're not compatible, but let's give ourselves a chance to find out.''

She didn't have that option. In spite of her longing, her feelings for him, his charm and persistence, she knew she had to keep her secret from him and send him packing back to Spain.

"I don't think that's a good idea.''

"You promised dinner tonight. I'm holding you to that.'' She gazed up at him, aware of his hand on her waist, his nearness, his green eyes filled with determination and a look that kept her pulse racing.

He brushed her lips lightly with a kiss and moved away. "I'll see you at seven, darlin'.'' He strode through her tiny apartment and opened the back door. "I doubt if that hamburger is fit to eat now. I'll feed you tonight.''

And then he was gone, and she stared at the closed door, frozen in shock over how once again she had capitulated to what he wanted. She heard the roar of the pickup. A pickup and cowboy boots and jeans. He had looked at home in them, but she knew better. He was a diplomat who lived in Europe and had spent nearly all his adult life abroad. He was First Secretary at the American Embassy in Spain. She could imagine the women he knew, beautiful, sophisticated—they didn't drop keys and carry hamburgers in their purses. She rubbed her temples and moved restlessly around the room. When he'd asked her out, all her resolve had just melted away. She was jelly where he was concerned, and she was going to have to do better tonight.

Why was she going? What would she wear? Was he doing this to sleep with her again? That question brought her up short and a flash of shame and anger burned in her.

She turned to a small mirror and shook her finger at her reflection. "Pamela, you were easy. Get a backbone where he is concerned! You'll have to send him packing tonight and stay cool, cool, cold."

She thought of guys who had called her frigid. Where was all that coldness she could turn on so easily with others?

She looked down at her flat stomach and splayed her fingers against it. A baby. Aaron's baby. He must never, never know. But in spite of the foolishness of getting pregnant in her first night of lovemaking, in spite of how it would turn her life upside down and in spite of all the struggles of being a single mother, she couldn't stop being thrilled and awed. Her own precious baby. Aaron's baby.

She knew from teaching the struggles the young single mothers and dads had, how they had to be everything for their kids and juggle jobs and schedules, but she would do it. Her own baby. Aaron's baby. This baby had a wonderful father.

Aaron has a right to know about his baby.

That thought was an unwanted one. He might have a right to know, but if he did, she knew he would want to do the right thing, and out of duty he would insist they marry. His family would hate her and think she had trapped him. No, he wasn't going to know, and he would marry some beautiful woman who was the right kind of woman for him and have his own family someday. She was certain of that. This was the only way it could be because Aaron would never be happy married to a woman like her. Not ever. And she didn't want duty or pity or charity. She couldn't bear to see him feeling trapped.

"Go to dinner and send him back to Spain. You know how to turn men off," she said and wondered when she had started talking out loud to herself and realized it had been since she met Aaron.

She threw up her hands and went to find something to wear

tonight. Her life had changed forever today—pregnant, dinner tonight with Aaron. He had come home to take her out! To get to know her better. A pang of longing made her tremble. Why did it have to be this way! "Because of my own carelessness," she answered herself.

Long ago she could remember Dr. Woodbury asking her if she wanted a prescription for the Pill and her turning him down, saying she wasn't dating and there was no need. When he had lectured her, she had turned a deaf ear. She should have listened, but then she touched her stomach again and knew she really had no regrets. She adored little children and this would be her own baby, something she had never dreamed possible.

Dinner with Aaron. If only— She shut her mind to following that line of thought, but she couldn't resist touching her throat and remembering his lips brushing against her.

Aaron whistled as he drove. He was excited, eager and he had to laugh at that hamburger stashed in her purse.

"No, darlin', I don't know any women like you and that's what's so wonderful about you. I like a country girl," he said out loud. It was refreshing to know she was going to tell him what she thought and not twist things all around or play games with him.

She couldn't believe he was here to take her out, but he would convince her. And maybe they wouldn't get along as well as he expected, but he had to find out. Maybe this was a bunch of foolishness on his part, but he knew he was excited, happy, and felt better than he had since the night of the gala.

At seven that evening his pulse raced while he stood at her front door and punched the bell. The door swung open and she smiled at him. His pulse jumped another notch at the sight of her. Her shiny black hair was short, straight, hanging loosely with the ends curling under just below her ears in a simple, uncomplicated hairdo that was like the rest of her. Her dress was an indigo sheath that clung to her slender figure. She didn't wear jewelry and had very little makeup, but she took his breath away, and, for an instant, he saw her without the dress, as he remembered her from that first night, slender, curvaceous, supple, warm, so damn giving and open to him.

"Hi," he said, his husky voice betraying what he was feeling.

"Come in," she said quietly, her blue eyes pulling him into their depths, and he wanted to say to hell with dinner and take her into his arms and straight to that tiny little virginal bedroom she had. Instead, he watched her as he walked inside. As soon as she closed the door, he turned to face her. He inhaled her perfume, a scent of lilacs, and it was an effort to keep from reaching for her, but he knew he'd better keep some kind of distance. The lady wasn't overwhelmed with eagerness to go out with him tonight.

"You look gorgeous."

"Thank you," she said, smiling with her cheeks flushing and a sparkle coming to her eyes that made him feel better. Why was she so solemn? She hadn't been that way that first night. He felt like he had done something wrong, but he couldn't imagine what.

"I'll get my coat. You look nice, too, Aaron, very elegant in your navy suit," she said shyly, and he couldn't keep from reaching out to brush her cheek lightly with his fingers.

"Thanks, darlin'. I've been getting ready for this date since I drove away from your place this afternoon."

She gave him an I-don't-believe-you look and turned to get her coat. He watched the gentle, sexy sway of her hips and tried to get his thoughts elsewhere because the slightest little thing with her could turn him on in a flash. For the first time he noticed the small elastic bandage that wrapped one slender ankle and he wondered if that was a lingering result of an injury during the rough landing of the Asterland jet.

His hands trembled slightly as he held her coat, brushing his fingers across her nape and trying to keep from taking her into his arms. She couldn't have any idea how badly he wanted her.

"You have a bandage on your ankle," he said when she

turned around to face him. Unable to keep from touching her, he smoothed the collar of her coat.

"I had torn ligaments in my ankle because of the plane's rough landing. I'm supposed to wear this bandage two more weeks. I thought about leaving it off tonight and seeing how I get along, but that might not be a good idea."

"Bandage or no bandage, your legs are beautiful. You wear it as long as you're supposed to," he said quietly, looking into her eyes while she gazed back at him and tension coiled between them.

"We should go, Aaron," she reminded him solemnly. He took her arm, still wondering about the barriers she had thrown up between them. When they left, she locked her apartment. He took her arm to walk to the car, looking at the flash of her shapely legs again as she slid into his black car.

When he entered the stream of traffic in the street in front of her apartment complex, Aaron glanced in the rearview mirror out of habit. He had spent years abroad, sometimes involved in intrigue, sometimes residing in countries that didn't welcome Americans, so he was accustomed to checking his surroundings and did it without thought. And, through habit, he noticed the black car turning into traffic a few cars behind him. When he got to Claire's, Royal's finest restaurant, instead of driving up immediately for valet parking, he circled the block.

"If you're looking for a parking spot, they have plenty in the back of their lot," Pamela said.

"Just driving around," he answered casually, aware she was watching him. In the rearview mirror, he saw the same black car turn the corner behind him, just as he turned another corner.

"I think we're being followed," he said, glancing at her to see what her reaction would be.

"Have you brought someone all the way from Spain to follow you around Royal, Texas?" she asked, her voice filled with disbelief. "Surely not!"

He turned back toward Main Street and slid to a stop at the

curb, knowing he was squarely in front of a fire hydrant, but he would be there only briefly. She didn't guess she might be the one being followed.

"No, darlin', I don't think so," he drawled, waiting. The car swung around the corner and had to pass him. He watched and pulled into the street behind the car.

The sedan had darkened windows, but when he drove behind it, he could see the silhouettes of two men. He noted the license tag, memorizing the number. At the corner they turned away from the restaurant and he turned toward it, driving up in front to let a valet park his car, but the incident worried him. He took her arm to walk to the front door of the restaurant.

"If they weren't following you—no one would be following a second-grade school teacher, Aaron. That's absurd."

"Maybe." He remembered talking to Justin about the site of the forced landing of the Asterland jet and all the questions the plane's malfunction had raised. Was Pamela in any danger? He reached out to open the door for her.

"You've spent too much time involved in European intrigue. You're in Royal, Texas, with a teacher from Royal Elementary. Nothing exciting here."

He stopped to face her, suddenly blocking her way. Startled, she looked up at him. *"Au contraire,"* he said solemnly, brushing her hair away from her cheek. "Being with you is the most excitement I've known in a long, long time."

"There you go again, pouring on charm thicker than molasses," she teased, making light of his statement, but her words sounded breathless and pink filled her cheeks.

"I mean it, lady," he said and moved out of her way, following her inside. He passed her to talk to the maitre d' and then they were ushered to a table with candlelight, a red rose in a crystal vase and a white linen tablecloth. When he ordered a bottle of French white wine, she interrupted.

"Aaron, I'll just drink water. I'm not much into wine or drinks."

She had been that night. She'd had wine at the gala and

another glass at his house. Maybe that had been a once-in-a-year thing. He knew so little about her, but he wanted to know everything. He ordered the wine for himself and water for her, wondering why everything she liked or said or did was so important to him.

"Do you like French food?" he asked. "If not, Chef Etienne does broil steaks—a concession to the steak-eating Texans. I know because I'm one of them."

She studied the fancy menu. "I see salmon that I'd like."

When their waiter returned for their order, Aaron said, "The lady will have the *saumon fumé avec pommes de terre primeurs au beurre de persil,*" he ordered in what sounded to her like flawless French. "I'll have a steak, medium rare, and a baked potato."

"You really do speak French fluently, don't you?" she asked as soon as they were alone.

"You make it sound like I rob gas stations often," he answered with a twinkle in his eye.

"Sorry. It's just another difference between us."

"Well, I won't converse with you in French, darlin'," he said, lapsing into a West Texas drawl.

She smiled slightly, but she didn't look happy.

"Believe me, we wouldn't be out together if there weren't differences between us," he said and she shrugged her shoulders slightly.

All through salads, his sizzling steak and her smoked salmon and new potatoes, he sensed a reserve in her that she hadn't had before. Something wasn't quite right, and he didn't know what it was. But when he looked into her guileless blue eyes, his heart raced. In their depths was desire.

He could feel that same volatile chemistry between them, that urgency that made sparks dance between them and kept him touching her lightly as often as possible. He wanted her in his arms, as close as possible. He wanted another night with her like the one they'd had. And he knew she was responding to his touches and looks. No matter how coolly she seemed to act, he could see her fiery response in her eyes. Buddies who knew he had taken her home the night of the gala had teased him unmercifully, talking about the ice maiden, the woman no man could touch. He'd learned about her mother. Justin had clued him in on that one, and he dimly remembered hearing things about Dolly Miles and the men who slept with her. Did that have something to do with Pamela's reserve? But Dolly Miles was of his parents' generation. Growing up, Aaron had paid little attention to rumors about Dolly Miles. He hadn't even known she'd a daughter, but Pamela was much younger than he was.

Over candlelight, he gazed at her, and for once couldn't eat much of a delicious steak. All he wanted was to devour the woman, looking regal and poised, sitting across from him. He even loved the smattering of freckles across her straight nose. And she was country in all the best ways, down-to-earth, practical. Except there was something she was holding back. He could sense it and there was no mistaking the cool reserve that held her in check most of the evening. Occasionally, he could bring forth a laugh and then the reserve was gone, and once she seemed to forget herself and reached over to grasp his wrist while she told him about a little boy in her second-grade class.

While he laughed with her, he was far more aware of her fingers holding his wrist. He twisted his hand around and grasped hers, raising it to his lips to brush a kiss across her knuckles. Instantly, she drew her breath and fires flickered in her gaze.

"Let's go home," he said in a husky voice and after a moment's hesitation, she nodded.

When she slipped her hand away from his, he motioned to their waiter. As soon as the waiter left them alone again, as Aaron put away his wallet, she touched his hand.

"Aaron, we rushed things before. I don't want to do that again."

He knew instantly what she was telling him, and he could not keep from being swamped with longing and disappointment. He wanted her in his arms again, bare to him, loving him totally, but lovemaking had to be the lady's choice. When he nodded solemnly, she looked relieved.

Was it her past? Her mother's reputation that she feared? Surely not. That was long ago. It had been her mother, not her. Pamela had a reputation for being circumspect and untouchable. Aaron certainly would do nothing to change that reputation either. He hadn't said a word about her spending the night at his house. His friends just knew they'd left the gala early together. Aaron had said he had taken her home and as far as townspeople were concerned, she was still Miss Untouchable, so how could it be that?

During the drive to her house, they both were quiet. He felt as if she was withdrawing from him, and he couldn't figure out why. While he thought about her, he was also watching to see if they were being followed. He couldn't pick up a tail, but when he went around the car to open her door, he thought he saw a movement in dark shadows to one side of her apartment building. He had a prickly gut feeling they were being watched, and he wished she had let him take her to his house, but he knew she wasn't going to.

Then, when he closed and locked the door behind her, he forgot about danger or being followed. As they entered her tiny living room, he reached out to slide her coat from her shoulders, letting his hands brush her neck.

He tossed her coat over a chair, placed both of his hands on her shoulders and studied her.

"What is it, Pamela? Something's changed."

"I'm shocked at your being here just to take me out," she answered, unable to look him in the eye, too aware of him, fighting her warring feelings. She wanted to close her eyes, stand on tiptoe and kiss him wildly. The evening had tightened the golden bands that bound her heart to him. She loved this tall, charming Texan desperately—and just as desperately, she knew she couldn't let him ever know about his baby.

He was a charmer, and she only half believed all his glib compliments. She knew she was out of her depth with him. She had to keep up her guard, but looking into his thickly lashed eyes, filled with intense desire, she knew keeping up barriers would be impossible with him.

"I asked you before, but I didn't get much of an answer so I want to ask again. Why were you gone before I woke that morning?" he asked quietly.

Three

Sooner or later she had known the question would come up again. She'd dreaded it, yet knew she had to face it and give him a reason for her flight. She met his questioning gaze squarely.

"I realized we had rushed into being intimate. That isn't like me, Aaron."

He stroked her hair away from her face. "I know that. You have a reputation for being very cool, very proper." As his voice dropped, his eyes darkened with desire that was so blatant, she could feel all her resistance melting away. "You gave me your virginity. I hope you don't have regrets. I don't have any. Far from it. I don't think we rushed anything—I think we followed our feelings. Mine haven't changed."

"Oh, Aaron," she whispered. How could she argue with him? How could she avoid telling him the truth? His questions were probing, difficult, and there was one way to end them. She moved the few inches closer to him, slipped her arm around his neck, stood on tiptoe and kissed him.

His arm banded her waist instantly. There was a husky growl deep in his throat as his mouth opened and his tongue thrust over hers, kissing her hungrily, pulling her tightly against him. He was rock hard, strong, lean and marvelous. She felt his arousal, felt her own body ache and tingle with longing.

Winding his hand in her hair, he tilted her head back, tightening his arm around her waist and bending over her so she had to cling to him while his kiss curled her toes and blocked out the world. Her pulse thundered in her ears, and she was aware only of Aaron and his kisses that scalded. Each stroke of his tongue over hers fanned the fires already blazing within her. She wanted him absolutely. Her hips thrust against him, need driving her and demolishing all her intentions of being cool.

He slid his hand down her back and his other hand slipped lower over her buttocks.

"Aaron," she whispered against his mouth, drowning in ecstasy and agony over being in his arms again.

"Why have you avoided me since the gala?" he asked, raising his head a fraction and studying her.

"I told you. I think we really rushed things."

"There's something you're holding back from me."

"Not this," she whispered and kissed him again, too aware that he knew something was dreadfully amiss. She had to keep him from learning the truth, but how could she hide anything from him?

Driving away her worries, his mouth covered hers and his kisses heated, conveying clearly that he wanted her. He swung her into his arms and moved to the sofa, sinking down with her cradled in his lap. One arm held her close while he kissed her. His other hand slipped lightly along her ribcage and then brushed across her breasts. She moaned softly, arching her back, and tightening her arms around his neck.

"Ah, lady, how I've dreamed of you, wanted you!"

The words were seduction; his kisses rapture. His fingers drifted over her nape, and then cool air brushed her back as he slowly tugged down her zipper. The coolness brought back a rush of resolutions and remembrance of her condition. She broke free and slipped off his lap, reaching around to try to pull up the zipper of her dress.

Aware of his heavy breathing and his piercing scrutiny, she slid to the other end of the sofa. "I want to stop," she said, knowing that wasn't what she wanted at all. She saw the desire in his eyes, and the questions. She had to get him out of her life. He was only amusing himself. Whatever drew him back to her was beyond her, but she knew, in spite of his smooth talk, it wasn't anything lasting. It couldn't be. Men like Aaron Black did not fall head over heels, instantly in love with second-grade school teachers from small West Texas towns.

"All right," he said, running his fingers along her knee and starting more tingles that battered her resolutions. "We'll just talk."

She couldn't tell him to go. She loved being with him and she gazed at him in silence, totally aware of his fingers moving on her knee.

"I think we were followed tonight. I don't suppose I can talk you into staying at my house—even in another bedroom. Just so you'll be safe."

Momentarily, her tension eased. She laughed and couldn't resist touching his hand lightly. He sat facing her, one long leg drawn up on the sofa. "No one is following me! And I'm perfectly safe here in Royal. No, I'm not spending the night at your house."

He gave her a long, direct look that erased her amusement. She realized he was in earnest. "No one knows why the Asterland jet had to make a forced landing."

"You think someone deliberately caused the plane's malfunction?" she asked, astonished. No question of sabotage had been raised in the papers. No one knew the cause of the jet's difficulties yet, but she had assumed an engine malfunction. "Surely not!"

"We don't know."

"I'm sure I'm safe. But I'll be careful."

"Promise you'll call me if there's anything that disturbs you."

"I promise," she said without giving it much thought, more focused on his steadfast gaze, aware of his fingers trailing above her knee now. "One thing that disturbed me since the crash, was the Asterland investigators. They came to ask me questions about the flight."

"They bothered you?"

"Don't look so fierce," she said, smiling at him and touching his cheek. "They were just too persistent with their questions."

"What did they ask you?"

"About what I was carrying on the plane, what my plans were for Asterland, if I had valuables with me. Forget it, Aaron. I don't want to think about them."

They talked until half past three, and then, when he rose to go, he pulled her into his arms again to kiss her long and hard. More kisses that conveyed that he wanted her with all his being. Kisses that made her melt and tremble and burn with need. His arms held her tightly against him and his tongue thrust deeply into her mouth, stroking her tongue. Suddenly he stopped and raised his head a fraction, bending down again to nibble kisses along her throat.

"Have breakfast with me," he said, trailing kisses to her ear, his tongue flicking over her ear. "Say yes, darlin'."

"Yes, oh, yes!" she said, her hands drifting over his back, wanting to touch him all over as she had that last time, wanting to feel his weight over her, feel him inside her again.

How she wanted him! He was as sexy and wonderful and exciting as she had thought he was that first night. Then she realized she had agreed to have breakfast with him, and that he had stopped kissing her. She opened her eyes to find him watching her with stormy green eyes.

"Pamela, anything your mother ever did doesn't have a damn thing to do with us," he said, and her heart thudded.

"I'm not like her," she whispered, wondering what he truly thought.

"I never once thought you were like anyone except your own special self," he said, leaning down to brush her lips lightly with his. His mouth was warm against hers, tantalizing. His words even more dazzling.

"I'm glad," she whispered. "So glad," she said, turning her mouth up to his for another long, searing kiss that she wanted to last forever. Too aware of her racing heart, his hot kisses, his long, lean body and strong arms, she clung to him until she knew she had to stop or there would be no stopping. She pushed against his chest and he raised his head. His breathing was ragged, and she could feel his heart pounding.

"I can be patient. I'll pick you up about eight. It was wonderful tonight, Pamela." He brushed another kiss across her lips and turned to the door and then paused. "Be careful, and if you want me anytime, just call. When I stay in town, I'm not that far away."

She nodded, barely hearing him, just wanting him so badly, memorizing everything about him. He shrugged into his coat and left. She stepped forward to slip the lock into place and leaned against the cool, hard wood, remembering Aaron's hot kisses, his hands moving over her.

"I want you, Aaron Black," she whispered, knowing she did want him with her whole heart. And knowing it was impossible to tell him.

She switched off lights and went to her bedroom, turning on the light, but standing frozen, lost in memories of the night. He knew something was amiss and not the same. He was too perceptive, too attuned to her feelings, and she wasn't accustomed to hiding the truth. He drifted in and out of that West Texas accent of his, reminding her there was another side to him and he wasn't a good ol' country boy. He was worldly, sophisticated, wealthy—everything she wasn't. She had to avoid being taken in by charm, glib words, hot sexy kisses.

"Aaron," she whispered. "Aaron."

Driving away, Aaron was hot, hard, tied in knots. Frustrated, still puzzled about Pamela's mixed signals, he wondered what was holding her back. Again, he wondered about hcr mother's reputation—if Pamela feared getting one like it. That seemed absurd, given that all the males who had ever mentioned her had talked about how cold and untouchable she was. Aaron drove out of the apartment lot, but on impulse, he went around a corner, cut the motor and climbed out. He turned his coat collar up and did as much as he could to hide his white shirt.

Moving into the shadows, he cut across yards until he was back at Pamela's apartment building. He circled one side of the building and, as he turned the back corner, he saw several things at once. She had a ground-floor apartment, and a light burned in her bedroom windows, escaping around the edges of the blinds. The dark silhouette of a tall man in a cap showed against the windows.

As Aaron moved forward, the man spun around and burst into a run.

Furious the bastard was window peeping or spying on Pamela, Aaron stretched out his long legs, but the man had a head start. Aaron was a runner, and he was closing the gap swiftly when thc man vaulted a fence. As Aaron leaped over the fence after him, the man jumped into a black car parked only yards away on a driveway.

When the motor roared to life, Aaron was just steps away. He lunged for the car, sprawling across the front fender.

The car raced backwards and Aaron couldn't gct a grip, his fingers sliding over the smooth hood before hc spilled off to the ground, but he saw two faces, one narrow with a long nose. The other face was a pale blur, much more square-shaped. The car whipped down the drive, turned into the street and, with a squeal of tires, was gone.

Aaron stood, brushing off his suit. He was certain it had been the same black car that had been following him before, and he'd got a dim glimpse of the two men inside. Total strangers. He worried about Pamela's safety. Someone was watching her, but who? And why?

Lost in thoughts about her and about thc man he had chased, Aaron drove home, checking his rearview mirror for a tail, but seeing no car trailing after him. Tomorrow he would trace the tag number on the car that had tailed them. It was Pamela who was being followed, and she obviously didn't have an inkling why.

At his Pine Valley house, Aaron stripped down and stretched out in his king-size bed. It would soon be time to get up, but sleep was as elusive as ever.

Lying awake in the dark of the large master bedroom, he wondered about the men following Pamela. Midmorning tomorrow, actually today, he had an appointment to meet with his friends, other members of the Texas Cattleman's Club. He thought about the old legend of Royal.

During the War with Mexico, jewels had been found and hidden in Royal. In 1910 when Tex Langley decided to establish the Texas Cattleman's Club, he and the founding members made a pact that only members of the Cattleman's Club would ever know of the jewels' true existence and members of the club would be the guardians of this town treasure, jewels that, according to the legend, were supposed to be the reason Royal prospered. The stones were kept in a treasure box, accessible to the club members via a secret passage under the original adobe mission built when Royal was founded. Now the mission was in Royal's large park by the Cattleman's Club.

Shortly after the Asterland jet had had to make the forced landing, four members from the Cattleman's Club had gone to the crash site, and Justin Webb had found two of the jewels—the black harlequin opal, the most valued of opals, and a two-carat emerald. All three jewels had to have been on that plane, but the third and most valuable, a red diamond, was still missing.

So far, the club members had kept things quiet, giving some of their information to Winona Raye, who was marrying Justin. A policewoman who worked with juveniles, Winona had agreed to be their contact with the authorities so they could keep things as quiet as possible and out of the media. The facts marched through Aaron's thoughts, taunting him with puzzle pieces that needed to be put together as quickly as possible. Someone out there was desperate. A trusted bartender, Riley Monroe, had been found dead near the mission where the jewels had been hidden. A scrap of a burned note found at the landing site didn't have enough written on it to piece together answers to questions. Robert Klimt, an Asterland cabinet member on the plane, was in a coma in the Royal Memorial Hospital, and the Cattleman's Club members wanted to talk to him to find out what he knew.

The priceless red diamond entrusted to the care of the Cattleman's Club members was missing and a man had been murdered. Two men were following Pamela. Plagued by concern for her safety, Aaron wished he had been more persuasive about her staying at his place. He wanted to let his friends know that Pamela was being followed. Others must be searching for the missing red diamond. Why were the jewels on the Asterland jet? Was it solely a jewel theft? The jewels were worth a fortune. Or were the jewels to be sold and the money to be used for some nefarious project? Who had killed Riley? Too many questions with too few answers, yet Aaron and his friends were dedicating their efforts to finding out.

He shifted restlessly. If he were staying out at the family ranch, he'd saddle up and ride because sleep wasn't coming anyway, but he couldn't do that here in town. And he wanted to be in town to be closer to Pamela and to his friends at the Cattleman's Club.

When they were needed, the members of the Texas Cattleman's Club worked together secretly to save innocents' lives—and now they seemed needed here in their own home town. Five of them were working on the jewel theft and the murder of Riley Monroe. Aaron stared into the darkness and ran through the list: Justin Webb, one of the Southwest's finest surgeons. Aaron's friend Matt Walker, local rancher. There was Sheikh Ben Rassad, rancher and horseman, and there was another longtime friend, retired Air Force, ex-Special Forces man, Dakota Lewis. Dakota gave him pause.

Aaron was a friend to both Dakota and his estranged wife,

Kathy Lewis. He had known Dakota most of his life and there had got to know Kathy when they were both in Washington, D.C., just starting in their careers. He had introduced Kathy to Dakota and the two had fallen wildly in love. Aaron had been shocked to hear of their breakup.

Once again, Aaron thought about all the men working on the theft. They had diverse occupations and backgrounds, but they all had had military experience, and now they were all able to take the time to solve the disappearance of the jewel and try to learn who murdered Riley Monroe—and why.

Aaron moved restlessly, his thoughts shifting to Pamela, memories taunting him. She was fighting her feelings, but the feelings were there and they showed sometimes. Like when she had stood on tiptoe and pulled his head down to kiss him. Just remembering made him respond physically as he became aroused.

Her true feelings were revealed in her responses to his kisses. All that cool reserve had gone up in flames, and she had all but come apart in his arms. But then she would become tense, pull back, and the barriers would come up again. Why?

The first gulf between them had opened that morning when she had slipped out of his house without his knowing it. The only reason he could figure had to be her feelings about her mother's reputation and shock over how swiftly she had yielded to him.

Yet he didn't have regrets. Far from it. That night had changed his life, and he felt to his bones that it had been important to her, too. And he intended to show her and try to get her back to that openness with him, that complete giving and honesty they'd had with each other the night of the gala. One step at a time.

Every time he searched his own feelings about her, he knew she was special. He was as tied up in knots as when he arrived in Royal. She had done nothing to alleviate that, far from it. He ached with wanting her. He wanted to make love to her all night long. The desolation he had lived with the past few years was gone now that he was home and seeing her again. Whatever it was that had come between them, he didn't think it would last or that it ran deep.

At least, come morning, he would have breakfast with her. Maybe he could talk her into staying at his place until they knew who was following her and why. Yeah, right, buddy, a cynical voice said. *You want the lady as close to your bed as possible.* So maybe he did, he admitted to himself. She felt something for him; he could see the longing in her eyes. She all but quivered at the slightest of his touches. And he really was concerned with her safety. He would bring his worries for her safety up again at breakfast, but the lady had a mind of her own.

What was disturbing her and holding her back? There was something going on in that pretty head of hers, some reason for the wall she was keeping between them. Before long he would have his answer. He intended to learn the truth about what was worrying her.

Promptly at eight the next morning, Pamela heard a motor and looked out to see a black pickup swing into the drive. A pickup during the day, a black sedan last night, a home in Pine Valley, one in Georgetown in Washington, one in Spain, the Black ranch here—while she rented a tiny apartment. Their lives were poles apart and she couldn't believe he was deeply interested in her. It seemed completely impossible.

As if unable to contain his energy, Aaron bounded out of the pickup and his long strides ate up the distance to the door. He was in boots, jeans and a plaid wool Western shirt and he looked like the other cowboys who lived around Royal. Only he wasn't like the other cowboys. In spite of his appearance and the West Texas drawl he could slip into so easily, she needed to remember that he led a far different life.

When he knocked on her door, she opened it and motioned to him to enter. She was too aware of his assessing gaze and the pleasure in his eyes as he took in her jeans and blue shirt. "Mornin', darlin'," he said quietly and stepped inside, bringing cold air in with him. "You look prettier than a prairie rose."

"Thanks, Aaron. I almost overslept."

"Wish I had been here to see you oversleeping," he said with a devilish twinkle in his green eyes.

"Well, it's best you weren't," she answered primly.

"Want to go back to catch a few winks?" he asked, swinging her up into his arms.

Startled, she yelped and put her arm around his neck. "No! Put me down, Aaron Black!"

"If you didn't get a good night's sleep, we can remedy that quickly." He headed toward her bedroom. "Just leave it to me, and you'll sleep like a baby."

"Don't you dare set foot in my bedroom. Put me down!" she said, laughing and knowing he was teasing as he headed toward her bedroom. He grinned and stopped.

"See—we can have a good time together."

"I know we can," she said, sobering, too aware how irresistible he was to her. She kept saying yes she would go out with him when she needed to avoid seeing him altogether. Yet he would be back in Spain so soon. She didn't really believe him about a leave of absence. And looking into his green eyes now while he held her in his arms, she tingled as he studied her in return.

"You handsome devil," she whispered, unable to keep from flirting with him.

He slowly lowered her feet to the floor, holding her so she was pressed against him. "Good mornin'," he whispered, and leaned down to kiss her, his mouth opening hers, his tongue stirring instant fires and driving all thought of sleep away. His strong arms held her tightly and in seconds her breathing was as erratic as his, her heart thudding violently.

Finally she broke away, pushing against his chest. "Aaron—you promised to take me to eat."

"Yeah, I did," he said in a husky voice, his gaze going over her features, his hand stroking her throat. He leaned down to kiss her throat and push open her shirt slightly to trail kisses lower. "I'd like to eat you," he whispered against her throat. "Kiss by slow kiss until you let go all that reserve." His warm fingers twisted free the top button of her shirt and he pushed it open, trailing kisses over the curve of her breast.

"Aaron," she whispered, her body growing taut, trembling with wanting to just let go and step into his arms and make love with him. Instead she put her hands against his chest that was as solid and hard as the wall. She pushed slightly.

He straightened up to stare at her solemnly. "I will, too, Pamela. Maybe not this morning, but you're going to be mine. You're pushing against me and saying no, but your blue eyes and your kisses are telling me something else."

"No, no!" She stepped back and buttoned her shirt. "Aaron, it's just impos—"

"Shh," he said, placing his fingers on her lips and then trailing them featherlightly over her mouth, teasing her while he stopped her argument. "C'mon, we'll go eat. We have time."

He helped her into her denim jacket, took her arm and they left to climb into his pickup. Dazed, all she could think was, no, they didn't have time. Time was against them. Definitely against them. They didn't have anything together. *You have a baby together,* a voice within her argued. She glanced at Aaron as he drove, looking at the angles and planes of his face, his prominent cheekbones and straight nose.

She should tell him about his baby. Yet she knew if she did, he would want to marry her because it was the right thing to do. Aaron Black was the kind of man honor bound to do his duty. She couldn't bear that. That night had meant something to him, too, but she couldn't believe it had really meant anything lasting or that she could begin to interest him like the other women he knew. Not even remotely. A second-grade teacher from Royal, Texas, being fascinating to an American diplomat stationed in Spain. Get real, Pamela, she told herself. She glanced at him and caught him studying the rearview mirror.

"Are we being followed again?"

"Nope. It's not easy to hide in Royal. In big-city traffic,

you can move into the flow of cars and get lost, but here, a tail sticks out like a heifer in a rose garden.''

"They have to be following you. There's no earthly reason to follow me.'' His eyebrow arched, but he remained quie and she wondered what was running through his mind. She realized how little she knew about him and suspected he coulc keep things to himself quite well. That arch of his brow in dicated he hadn't agreed with her, but why would anyone fol low her?

He turned to park in front of the Royal Diner and cam around to hold the door open for her. "You're not wearing coat. Don't you get cold?'' she asked, pulling her denim jacke closer as a gust of wind hit them.

"Nope,'' he said, draping his arm casually across her shoul ders and drawing her close against his side. "I've got yo here to keep me warm.''

She smiled at him and couldn't keep from liking his holdin her close against him. She was five feet ten inches, tall for woman, but Aaron was six feet four inches and he made he feel smaller and dainty, something she rarely experienced.

He swung open the diner door and the bell tinkled as the stepped into the warmth of the café. The windows wer steamed, and smells of frying sausages and eggs and hot coffe assailed her. Before they reached a booth, Pamela knew sh had made a mistake in accepting this date.

Too many mornings she couldn't keep anything down, bu she'd thought if she ate lightly and was careful what she ate she would be all right, and she had wanted to be with hir one more time. But, as they slid into a booth and smells o frying foods assailed her, her stomach became queasy. Sh wouldn't be able to eat a bite, and what excuse could she giv him?

"Something wrong?'' he asked, and she flicked him glance. Those damnable green eyes were searching her face and she wished he couldn't read her so easily. No one els could, yet he seemed to see what was running in her mind an guess what her feelings were intuitively, and that unnerved her, too.

"I'm all right," she said, feeling worse by the minute. Why had she come? Why was he so darned irresistible to her? Sheila approached.

"Good morning, Aaron, Pamela," she said, looking back and forth between them as if she couldn't believe her eyes. "What'll y'all have? Orange juice, coffee, tomato juice, something to start? Manny's cooking flapjacks and biscuits and gravy this morning."

Aaron looked at Pamela and frowned slightly, bending his head to really study her. Her stomach was churning now. She shook her head slightly, unable to say a word. The thought of any food turned her stomach.

"Why don't you bring two orange juices and one coffee, Sheila," Aaron said without taking his eyes from Pamela.

The moment the waitress was gone, Pamela knew she had to get out of the diner and away from the smells. She needed some cold air, too.

"Excuse me," she said as she slid out of the booth and dashed for the door. Embarrassment and anger at herself for coming with him flooded her. She should have known better. Eight mornings out of ten she lost her breakfast. Why, oh why did she let him talk her into anything and everything? Her stomach heaved and she knew she was going to be sick, and if she lost it here in the diner   oh, horrors! The rumors that would start.

Rumors that would be true.

She was fumbling for the door when a long arm shot past her and opened it. She rushed outside, too aware Aaron was right beside her. She hurried away from the diner toward his pickup, grasping the door handle as she lost everything. Her stomach heaved, and embarrassment made her want to curl up and faint. If only she could!

He thrust a clean handkerchief under her nose.

"I'm sorry," she said, unable to look at him.

"You should have told me if you didn't feel all right," he

said. "Let me take you to a doctor. You might be getting tⁱ
flu." He felt her forehead and to her horror, she gagged agaiⁱ

"Oh, Aaron, I'm sorry," she said, wishing with all her bⁱ
ing that she was a million miles away from here. Or that ⁱ
was a million miles away. Why couldn't he have stayed ⁱ
Spain!

"Stop apologizing for being sick. Happens to all of uⁱ
Want to sit in the truck?"

"Yes," she said, thankful the windows of the diner weⁱ
steamed up and had curtains, and that the street was almoⁱ
deserted at eight in the morning so few people were witnessiⁱ
her nausea.

He opened the door, picked her up and lifted her inside. ⁱ
can get in by myself," she protested.

"You don't need to now," he answered, closed the doⁱ
and walked around the pickup to slide in on the other sidⁱ
"Want the heater on?"

"No. The cold air feels better."

He felt her forehead again. "You don't feel feverish, bⁱ
several people in town have the flu. Doc Williams is my doⁱ
tor, and I'm sure I can get you in to see him."

"No! I don't need a doctor."

"It won't hurt," he said, starting the motor, and she paⁱ
icked.

"No! This isn't anything unusual and it isn't the flu. I doⁱ
want to go see your doctor. I don't need to. Just take me homⁱ
Aaron." The words burst from her because she knew how ⁱ
took charge and did what he wanted.

"You've been sick before?" he asked.

"Sometimes," she said. "It passes. I don't need to see yoⁱ
doctor. I'd like to go home," she said, talking fast. She wipⁱ
her brow and leaned back against the seat with her eyes closeⁱ
As her stomach began to settle, she became aware of the ⁱ
lence. She glanced at him to find him looking at her so intenⁱ
that her breath caught.

"How often have you been sick before?" he asked quietⁱ

and then she realized she had blurted out too much. Aaron paid attention to every little thing.

"It's nothing. I have a delicate stomach."

"Since when?"

"You don't know what I have. I need to go home," she said, avoiding answering him and aware she was being evasive, which stabbed at her conscience.

He turned and started the motor and backed out. They drove in silence, and she couldn't wait to get home and away from his scrutiny. She vowed that she would never accept another breakfast date again with him. No more dates with him, period.

He pulled up in front of her apartment complex and climbed out. At her front door she turned to him. "I'm sorry, but thanks for being so understanding."

He took the key from her hand and unlocked her door, pushing it open and waiting for her to go inside.

"Aaron, I think I need to be alone."

"I won't be here long," he said, taking her arm and going inside. He kicked the door closed behind him and slipped her jacket off her shoulders, tossing it over a chair and leading her to her sofa. "Want anything?"

"No, thanks. Really, I'm fine." She didn't want him coming in with her and she didn't like the way he was looking at her, studying her as if he were getting ready to dissect her.

"Want to sit down?" he asked her. Her uneasiness was growing with each second and the way he was staring.

She sat and moved back against the corner of the sofa, closing her eyes and wishing he would disappear. What was running through his mind?

She felt him sit close to her and she knew if she opened her eyes, she would find him still studying her. She said a small prayer that Aaron couldn't possibly guess what was really wrong with her.

"How many mornings have you been sick?" he asked quietly, and her eyes flew open.

Frightened that he had guessed her secret, she stood and

moved away from him, feeling as if he knew her ever
thought. "A few."

She heard him move and then his hands settled on he
shoulders. When he turned her to face him, his green eye
were stormy.

"You're pregnant."

She couldn't lie and deny it. "I should never have gone t
breakfast with you." The words spilled out of her and sh
wrung her fingers together. She wanted to deny his accusatio
to get him out of her apartment, but she couldn't lie to him
so she just kept talking in circles around his statement. "I fe
queasy this morning. I never could take fried food early in th
day very well," she said, trying to twist away from him, bu
his hands held her firmly.

He bent his knees to lean down and look into her eyes wit
a gaze that pierced to her soul. "*Are* you pregnant, Pamela?

Four

She couldn't answer and she couldn't lie, so she merely nodded.

"You're pregnant with my baby." His eyes widened, and the color drained from his face. "Lordy!" he whispered under his breath, looking incredibly shocked.

"Aaron, this isn't your problem. Just leave me alone and I'll take care of it." Humiliation, anger, protectiveness, all three emotions churned in her like a stormy sea as she watched his shock grow.

"I thought you said you were protected," he said.

A flush burned her cheeks. "Well, I wasn't. That's my mistake, and I'll take care of it." Anger at herself and with him fueled the fires she was suffering. She just wanted him out of her house. "This isn't your problem, Aaron." Closing her eyes, she bit her lip while all her worries about his discovery of the truth crashed in on her.

Staring at her, Aaron was shocked because, even though they were in the throes of passion, he had accepted her "yes," that night that she was protected. A baby. *Their baby.* He was stunned. Always methodical, he had planned his college years, planned his years with the State Department and, in the back of his mind, he had planned to someday marry and have a family. He had figured on a wedding before a baby.

He was shocked, but realized that this pregnancy was what had been disturbing her. He came out of his fog of surprise and looked at her. Her cheeks were flushed, tears brimmed in her eyes and she was wringing her hands together, and he realized in his momentary shock, he wasn't treating her the way he should.

"Aw, Pamela," he said, tenderness and wonder filling him. They were going to have a baby! This pregnancy wasn't the way he had planned his future, but she had to be very early in her pregnancy. They could have a wedding, and everything would be right. "Darlin'," he said, stepping close to wrap her in his arms. "We'll have a wedding right away."

"No!" she said, wriggling away from him, startling him again. She was stiff and unreceptive, and now when he looked at her, her blue eyes blazed.

"Look, I'm sorry," he said gently. "I was just surprised. I want to get married—"

"No, Aaron. We're not having a wedding. I'm the one to blame for this—"

"Well, I sort of think it took two of us," he drawled, frowning and seeing he would have to mend his fences quickly.

"No, I should have been responsible and I wasn't. This isn't your problem—"

"Pamela! Our baby isn't a *problem,*" he interrupted, suddenly terrified she was thinking of abortion. "You can't harm this baby!" he snapped, wondering if he knew her after all.

While all color drained from her face, she trembled, and with relief he knew he had been wrong on that score.

"I would never knowingly harm my baby," she said fiercely, placing her hands in front of her flat tummy.

"Hell, I'm going about this all wrong," he said. "It's my baby, too, and I want to marry you."

When she closed her eyes as if he had struck her, he felt at a loss. "No."

"What am I doing wrong here?" he asked, puzzled and realizing something was terribly amiss between them. Yet she had gone out with him and she had responded to his kisses. He glanced past her at the small clock on her mantel. He had an appointment to meet his friends at the Texas Cattleman's Club soon. They'd just have to go on without him, though, because this was more important.

Her blue eyes opened and were as fiery as ever. If looks could have flattened him or sent him running, hers would have. "You're not doing anything wrong. You just need to realize that you don't have to marry me. I did this and I want my baby and I'll give this baby all the love possible, but you're not part of this."

"The hell I'm not," he said, realizing she was in earnest. "That's my baby, too."

"Aaron, did you think you'd get married someday?"

"Yes, of course."

"And you imagined a big wedding with your family and friends, didn't you?"

"Yes, I did," he said evenly. "But it's not too late for that. With the money I have we can pull a big wedding together quickly," he said, for one of the few times in his life mentioning the wealth he had inherited.

"No. You go on with your life the way you planned it. You'll find a woman who is your type, who lives the lifestyle you do and has your family's approval. When you find her, you'll marry and have your own family and you'll be very happy. I appreciate your asking me to marry you, but I knew you would do that because you're a good person. I want love in my marriage and we don't share love. No, I won't marry you."

"That's bull, Pamela," he said. "I'm back here in Royal because I wanted to be with you."

"The night we had was magic, but it was sex, and sex turns men's heads. You're not thinking about this clearly. Your goodness and your emotions are running away with you. When you calm down and get accustomed to the idea, you'll agree with me.''

"The hell I will," he said quietly. He wanted to pull her into his arms, but she had put invisible barriers between them and he could see the stiffness in her shoulders. Her chin was in the air as if she were getting ready to go into a fight, and her eyes still blazed with anger.

"I saw your first reaction," she accused.

"I was just shocked. And I wasn't thinking."

"Oh, yes, you were. Those were your true feelings."

"I'd like to kiss all those foolish notions about me right out of your head." As he moved closer, she stepped back and held up her hand.

"You're not going to! Don't you kiss me."

"Darlin'," he said gently, "you're upset and emotional and reading my feelings all wrong. This won't be a shotgun wedding."

She waved her hand. "Aaron, look around you. We're totally different. I rent this little apartment. I've hardly traveled away from Royal. You have homes all over the world—Washington, D.C., Spain, here. The women you date are sophisticated and from your world."

"I don't want to date them, and you're selling yourself short. The women I know are sophisticated and some of them want things I don't want and value things I don't value. Some of them are tough and ambitious to the point of putting that first in their lives."

"Haven't you done exactly that with your work? Aren't you very ambitious?"

"Yes, I am," he admitted, "but I don't want to marry someone who is ambitious above all else."

"You can't tell me you've never been attracted to any of the women you've known!" she snapped, sounding more annoyed with him.

"Of course, I have, but I've never found anyone who

wouldn't get out of my thoughts or who seemed so right to be with or who made me feel like a human being again."

She drew a deep breath and looked shaken, and he felt a degree better until she shook her head. "No. I think you're getting desire and lust all mixed up. Men are driven by what their bodies want. Your heart has little to do with what is going on between us."

"I don't—"

As the doorbell jangled, Aaron swore under his breath. "Ignore it and they'll go away," he said, but she was already walking away from him. Trailing after her, he clenched his fists and knew he was going to have a fight on his hands. He wanted to kick himself for not hiding his shock. He knew better, and no matter how shocking the news had been, never in his career had he let his feelings be exposed like that. But this was different. The realization that he would be a father ran much deeper than diplomacy and politics. His relationship with Pamela involved his whole heart and life.

He wished to hell he could take back the first moment he'd found out. He suspected his lady had already made her mind up about their baby and no matter what he had done, it would have been the wrong thing.

When she swung open the front door, three little girls faced her.

"Hi, girls."

"Can you play, Mellie?" the oldest one asked.

Pamela glanced over her shoulder at him. "Yes, I can," she said coolly. "Come inside, and I'll introduce you to my friend."

"Pamela!" a woman called.

She stepped outside, and Aaron could hear a woman's voice and guessed it was their mother. "Do you mind? Is this a bad time for them to come over?"

"No, it's fine. I'll bring them home in about an hour."

"Sure?"

"Yes, I'm sure," she answered firmly, and Aaron knew she was getting rid of him. Three towheaded little girls with large brown eyes stared at him as if he had dropped from Mars. He tried to smile at them, but he wished they would come back in an hour and let him finish talking to Pamela.

She closed the door and turned to face him, looking satisfied that she had found a quick end to their conversation. "Aaron, these are my neighbors, Hannah, Rachel and Ellen Colworth. Girls, this is Mr. Black."

"Hi," he said, and they solemnly said hi to him and then the oldest turned to Pamela.

"Can you read to us?"

"I surely can. Mr. Black was just leaving. Unless you want to stay around and listen to *Peter Rabbit* and *Goldilocks and the Three Bears*.

"We'll get the books," Hannah said, and the three of them scampered toward her bedroom.

"You do this often?" he asked, realizing she was good with children.

"They're my preschool neighbors and they like to come play. They have a new baby in the family, and it gives their mother a break."

"Mellie?"

"They can't pronounce Pamela."

"Okay, you get out of this conversation for now, but I'm not finished."

"We are finished, Aaron," she answered so solemnly that his heart clenched.

"No, we're not. I want to take you to dinner tonight."

"No—"

He was tired of the foolish arguments when he knew from her kisses and responses that there was something good and true between them. He stepped forward swiftly, wrapped his arms around her and kissed away her negative reply.

She pushed against him, but he leaned over her and kissed her hard and deep and with all the hunger, conviction and longing he had pent up in him. As their tongues tangled and clashed, she yielded to him and then responded. Knowing that at any minute the children could return and interrupt them, he raised his head.

"I'll pick you up at half past seven. All right?" He could see her coming out of her daze. Her lips were red from his kisses, her eyes burned now with different fires. His pulse jumped because there had to be more than a strong attraction between them for her to react so swiftly and intensely to him. "Say yes or I'll kiss you senseless, girls or no girls."

Pamela stared at him, knowing she had to refuse, yet knowing he was going to win this argument. "Arguing more tonight won't do you any good."

"Don't care. Is half past seven all right?" As he leaned down and his mouth touched hers, his tongue touching her lips, she twisted away.

"Yes! You know what you can do to me," she accused as he straightened and stepped away, but he kept his hand on her waist. With his other hand he touched her cheek.

"Has it occurred to you that maybe your reaction to my kisses is because of the depth of feelings between us?"

"We don't know each other that well. That first night we were together had to be physical attraction, pure and simple."

He wound his fingers in her hair and stared at her while he shook his head. "It went deeper than that or I'd be in Spain right now."

"Mellie!" Hannah called, and he glanced around to see the little girls standing a few yards behind him with books in their arms.

"I'll go now, but I'll see you tonight."

"A dinner date won't change a thing."

"We'll see, darlin'," he drawled and leaned forward to kiss her lightly.

"Now your kiss will raise questions from the girls."

He turned to go out the back door and paused when he reached the little girls who were staring at him. "What books will she read to you?" he asked, hunkering down in front of the oldest child.

"We want her to read all these. I like *The Three Little Pigs* and Rachel likes *Goldilocks* and Ellen likes *Billy Goats*."

"Good choices. It was nice to meet all of you. I'm going now, and Mellie can read to you. Have fun."

Hannah nodded solemnly as he stood and turned to Pamela. "I'll let myself out. See you tonight."

She watched him stride through the house and she wanted to let go the tears she fought to hold back, but she couldn't cry in front of the girls. Instead, she tried to close her mind to Aaron and his proposal and his arguments. She smiled at the girls. "Ready to read?"

"Are you crying?" Hannah asked bluntly.

Pamela swiped at her eyes. "Not really. Let's sit on the sofa." She sat down and let Ellen climb into her lap while Hannah and Rachel crowded close beside her, and she picked up the first book to start to read. She was going out with him again tonight. Why couldn't she just say no and stick with it? She knew why—she thought of his hot kisses that drove every rational thought from her head. The chemistry between them was incredible, no denying that. Her mouth still tingled, and she ached with longing to just let go and give herself to him again. She longed to accept his proposal—

She stopped her thoughts from continuing down that track because she knew that kind of forced marriage would never work. Not when they were so different and knew each other so little. No matter how painful it had been, she had done the right thing. And she had to make him see that he wasn't being realistic about marriage. When the town found out about her pregnancy, gossip would begin linking her to her mother's behavior and she didn't want Aaron pulled into that ugliness.

She tried to focus on the book in her lap and forget Aaron.

Aaron entered the bar of the Texas Cattleman's Club and strode across to a private room where he joined his friends, shaking hands with his longtime friend Dakota Lewis.

"Your hand doesn't feel like ice," Dakota teased, "but I'll bet you're late because you've been with the teacher."

"As a matter of fact, I have," Aaron admitted, greeting Matt Walker, Justin Webb and Sheikh Ben Rassad. "I've been eager to get here because we have a new problem." Aaron sank down onto one of the leather chairs and stretched his long legs in front of him. "There are two investigators here from Asterland."

"Garth Johannes and Milo Yungst," Matt Walker said, sitting on a sofa and propping his elbows on his knees.

"You know about them. They questioned Pamela and shook her up," Aaron said.

"They've wanted to talk to Lady Helena, but so far, the hospital has refused to let them. They shouldn't be aggressive with these women," the rancher remarked. "Did you tell Pamela about the jewels?"

"No," Aaron answered. "Not because I don't trust her. I just think she might be safer knowing as little as possible about what's happened. I'd like to keep her out of it as long as I can."

"Good idea," Justin added with a grim note in his voice, and Aaron wondered if the physician was concerned about the safety of his fiancée Winona Raye, since she was involved as their liaison with the police.

"There's something else," Aaron said. "Two men are following Pamela. I don't know whether Johannes and Yungst are tailing her or if the men following her are hired guns." He went on to tell his friends about chasing the man who had been watching her apartment.

"Did you get a good look at them?" Justin asked.

"The one I chased is tall and thin. Then, as I hit the car, I glimpsed them. Oval face, long nose—the other looked square. It was too dark to get anything definite."

"Sounds like the investigators," Justin said. "Winona and I saw them at Claire's."

"I traced the license-tag number and it was a car stolen over a year ago, later found stripped and burned with the tag missing. A dead end there," Aaron said. "I want to know why they're following her. Do they think she was involved some way in whatever caused the forced landing? Do they think she has the red diamond?'' Aaron asked, mulling over his questions aloud. While he talked, his thoughts were just partly on the mystery. Part of his thoughts kept returning to Pamela and her news of their baby. He couldn't get her pregnancy out of his mind. He thought about Justin who was getting married and adopting a baby girl. A wife and a baby. The idea was awesome and breathtaking. He wished he could talk to Justin about how it felt to become a father, but his fatherhood had to stay a secret at this point in his life. Glancing at the doctor, Aaron realized Justin was talking, so he tried to focus on what his friend was saying.

"The women who were on the plane may be in danger," Justin said. "If the Asterland investigators are following Pamela, they may be watching Lady Helena, too."

Aaron's concern deepened because Justin was probably right. The women could be in a lot of danger. "I think we should keep a watch on the women who were on the plane," Aaron said. "I'll watch Pamela because I'll be with her anyway."

"I can guard Lady Helena," Matt said quietly, his green eyes were cold as he met Aaron's gaze. "I know Anna and Greg Hunt plan to take her home with them when she can be released, but until then, I'll stand guard."

"Jamie Morris stayed behind in Royal instead of going on to Asterland on the next flight," Justin added. "She was on her way to an arranged marriage to a member of Asterland's Royal Cabinet."

"I wonder why she stayed in town. Whatever the reason she is still here, she was also on the Asterland jet and may need protection," Aaron said. "How about you, Ben?" He looked at the sheikh who frowned. Dressed in his robes and kaffiyeh, he stood out from the rest of them.

"If she is in danger, I will do this," he replied, nodding solemnly.

"How about Dakota keeping tabs on the investigators?"

Matt asked, and all heads turned toward the tough male who was estranged from his wife. He nodded.

"Sure. I'd like to catch them following someone."

"Klimt's in a coma," Matt said. "The diamond is missing, and we're no closer to a reason why the stones were on the plane or why the plane went down."

"Someone has the missing red diamond, but evidently it isn't anyone connected officially with Asterland or their investigators wouldn't be quizzing the women so much about the jewelry they were carrying on the plane," Aaron said, remembering all Pamela had told him about their questioning.

"None of the federal investigators of the crash have come up with the reason yet for the forced landing," Justin said. Standing by a window, he stared outside. "As soon as they do, we'll know a little more than we do now."

"So we still don't know if the forced landing had something to do with the missing jewels," Aaron said.

"No, and the police are as baffled as we are about Riley Monroe's murder," Justin added. "Who killed him?"

"When we know that," Aaron said, "we'll know what they intended to do with the jewels. Was it a theft for the fortune they would bring, or were the stones intended for someone or some purpose in Asterland since they were found on the jet headed to Asterland?" He glanced at Justin. "You have them safely hidden?"

"Yep, they're behind our plaque in the front entrance hall."

"Leadership, justice and peace," Ben said quietly. Aaron knew the stones represented each of these three qualities, a mantra for the Cattleman's Club members to uphold and the words carved into the plaque.

The men sat and talked for another half an hour about various topics—how the Cowboys' football season had gone, how it should shape up next fall, until finally Aaron stood and said he needed to go.

Matt was on his feet instantly, saying he had to get to Royal Memorial to guard Lady Helena.

As they stood, before they broke up their group, they once

again went over the questions in a reminder of the problems facing them.

"We've got one murder and one missing diamond." Justin added, "The women may be in danger. We don't want anything else bad happening and we need to find the red diamond."

"See you later," Aaron said, leaving the club and already thinking about his date that night with Pamela.

As they walked outside, Matt fell into step beside him. "If those bastards try to harm Lady Helena after all she's been through—they'll have to go through me to get to her."

"I've started carrying my gun," Aaron said solemnly. "I'm worried about Pamela's safety."

"Yeah, well, now with Ben watching Jamie and Justin trying to keep an eye on Winona and Dakota following those investigators, maybe everyone will be safe."

"If I can talk her into it, I'm taking Pamela to my house tonight."

Matt arched his brow and gave him a look. "Good idea. She'll be safer there. Taking her to the ranch?"

"No, we'll stay in Pine Valley. I don't think I can get her to go out to the ranch. She's accustomed to living in town."

"It would be easier to protect her at the ranch."

"The lady is going to make up her own mind about it. That's for sure."

"Yeah, they have a way of doing that. Be careful."

"You, too. I think Pamela wants to go to the hospital to see Lady Helena so you'll probably see us tonight or tomorrow night."

"Good. Pamela's great, Aaron. I've known her a long time and a lot of people let all that crummy stuff about Dolly color their feelings about Pamela, but she's a good person and damned nice."

"I think so, too. I want to marry her."

Matt nodded. "Good."

He turned away and Aaron headed to his car. She was carrying their baby. The more he thought about it, the more awesome and wonderful her pregnancy was. She was so mistaken about his feelings. But they'd talk it out tonight. Whistling, his spirits lifted as he looked in his rearview mirror to see whether or not he was being followed.

The minute Pamela swung open the door that night, Aaron knew he was in for a battle and some fast talking. Standing stiffly facing him, she took his breath in spite of the fiery stubbornness flashing in her eyes. A simple red dress clung to her slender figure like a scarlet flame. She so often wore clothes that covered her to the chin, but nonetheless she exuded a sexy air that kept him hot and disturbed.

"This dinner date is just ridiculous," she said.

When he stepped inside, she moved back to let him pass, but he could see her reluctance before she turned to go get her coat and purse.

He inhaled her lilac perfume and looked at the satiny highlights in her hair, which swung slightly as she walked ahead of him. He watched the pull of the skirt across her hips. A zipper ran from the neck down below her bottom and he wanted to tug it down and peel her out of the dress. He knew he'd better keep his mind on the problems between them because he suspected it was going to take some of his best powers of persuasion to convince her of his feelings.

She turned to face him and folded her arms across her middle, looking challenging and stubborn and beautiful. "This is so silly for us to go to dinner. We'll spend the evening arguing."

"Well, then, we won't argue," he said cheerfully, picking up her coat. "You have to eat, so you might as well go with me and have a scrumptious dinner at Claire's and we can talk about any subject you want."

"That's just putting off the inevitable."

"It won't hurt to put it off until after dinner." He held her black coat out for her to slip into, and they stared at each other over it.

"You look beautiful," he said, his voice lowering a notch.

She seemed exasperated by his compliment and thrust her arm into her sleeve. He slipped the coat onto her shoulders and lifted her hair out of the way, brushing her nape slowly with his fingers.

"Stop flirting, Aaron," she said darkly.

"Impossible when I'm with you," he whispered at her ear and then brushed a light kiss across her cheek.

Turning to slant an angry look over her shoulder at him, she clamped her lips together. He could almost see her refusal to go out surfacing, so he took her arm and spoke quickly as he steered her to the door. "I told my brother Jeb about you. He has a second-grader, my little nephew Robby. He's having trouble with his reading. Can I tell my sister-in-law she can call you and talk to you about Robby?"

"Of course."

"They have Robby in a private school, and they've had a tutor, but something isn't working right."

"Have they had him tested for dyslexia? I'm sure they have," she answered her own question swiftly. "I can't imagine with all the individual attention, he doesn't get the help he needs."

Aaron held open the door, locking it behind them and looking around as they stepped outside. He didn't want Pamela to know he was carrying a gun now. If he gave chase to anyone again, he was going to be able to stop a car from getting away. And he worried about Pamela's safety.

He didn't see anyone lurking in the shadows, but once they were on Main Street, he spotted a tail again. Picking up his phone, he called Dakota to inform him of the black car and learned that Dakota already knew about it. As soon as he broke the connection, Pamela spoke.

"You're being followed again. Aaron, what are you involved in that someone would follow you? You're halfway around the world from Spain."

"I don't think I'm the one who's being followed."

"Not me! You're so wrong there."

"Those two investigators from Asterland were persistent in

their questions and were with you for over an hour, weren't they?''

"Yes. You think they're following me?" She twisted around in the seat to glance out the back.

"The investigators seem a likely possibility. If you're trying to see them, the men following are two cars behind us."

Turning to face him again, she settled in the seat. "I'm sure you're the one they're interested in. There's no reason to follow me."

He reached Claire's and turned into the lot for valet parking, climbing out of the car and glancing at the street, but he couldn't spot the tail and he wondered if they had turned off before the restaurant.

The maitre d' greeted Aaron and led them to a table near a quiet corner of the restaurant.

"Now I know why you aren't drinking any wine."

Reflected candlelight flickered in the depths of her luminous blue eyes that were so large, he felt enveloped in blue. "It wouldn't be good for the baby," she said quietly.

He nodded and looked up as the waiter stopped at their table. "Good evening, Miss Miles, Mr. Black," he said. "Would you like to see our wine list? Tonight we have a special French red wine."

"I'll take a glass of the red wine, and the lady will have water," Aaron replied. As soon as they were alone, he asked her, "Who's your doctor?"

"I went to my family doctor, Dr. Woodbury."

"You should have a specialist."

"I'm going to change because I got a call today from Dr. Woodbury's nurse and he's retiring. They're notifying his regular patients, so I called and made an appointment with an obstetrician."

"Good. I could ask Justin who he recommends."

"No, you don't. I'll decide which doctor I go to."

Aaron rubbed his cheek and nodded, suspecting he wouldn't get anywhere with an argument. "Who's the doctor you have an appointment with?"

"Dr. Burke."

"Ahh. Leon Burke?"

"Yes. I take it from your 'ahh' that you approve of my choice?"

"My sister knows him and thinks he's a good doctor. I've heard her talk about him. Yes, I approve."

She rubbed her forehead. "Whether you approve or not, Aaron, this is my choice of doctors."

"Sure, darlin'. Are you still planning to do substitute teaching?"

"Yes, I enjoy teaching and I can keep busy with substituting. Actually, I haven't signed up to sub yet because I was waiting for my ankle to heal. When I teach, I'm on my feet most of the day, but I'm able to do that now, I think."

"Which school will you teach in?"

He listened, steering the conversation away from anything personal while they were served drinks and later were served their dinners. At first she was stiff and remote, but gradually she relaxed somewhat, although she was still guarded. She seemed to have as little appetite as he did.

"You're barely eating. That can't be good."

She shrugged. "It won't last. I just don't feel hungry tonight."

Neither did he. Placing his fork in his plate, he reached across the table to take her hand, holding it lightly in his. "I want to marry you."

She shook her head. "Thank you, Aaron, but no. I want to marry for love. How many times have you said, 'I love you' to me? Or have I said it to you?" Before he could reply, she spoke again. "Don't declare your love now. You haven't said 'I love you' to me because you don't love me."

"I think I am in love."

"Oh, please, Aaron! You're doing what you think is right."

"No, I'm not," he replied and it hurt him to see the pain in her blue eyes. He ached to pull her into his arms and convince her to marry him.

"Aaron, I saw the look on your face when you realized I was pregnant. It wasn't joy."

"No, it was surprise," he admitted honestly. He leaned forward. "How did you learn that you're pregnant?"

"Dr. Woodbury told me."

"And wasn't your first reaction surprise?"

She gave him another exasperated look.

"Answer me, Pamela. Wasn't your first reaction surprise?"

"Maybe it was, but it didn't last long."

"Neither did my surprise. But you can't hold surprise against me when that was the exact same reaction you had."

She stood abruptly. "I want to go home."

He knew he had gotten to her on the last. He held her coat for her and draped his arm across her shoulders as they left the restaurant.

In the car Pamela sat with her arms crossed tightly in front of her. They were going back to her apartment, and she knew they would have another battle and this time the little girls wouldn't interrupt and end it. She glanced at Aaron. He could be so darned persuasive! But when she thought of the future, she knew she was right. He wasn't really in love. Never once had a declaration of love crossed his lips. It might now, but she wouldn't believe it. She just needed to stand firm and then he would go on his way and that would be that.

As he drove, she watched him. His hands were well-shaped, blunt fingers with nails trimmed short. He was handsome, intelligent, the best daddy for her baby.

He glanced in the rearview mirror.

"Are we being followed?" she asked.

"No, we're not."

She couldn't imagine he was right about anyone following her. Why would someone follow her? She didn't have anything valuable. As they approached her apartment, a muscle worked in his jaw, and her pulse raced. She knew he would finally have to come to grips with her decision. This would be their last date. He would kiss her. Anticipation made her pulse fly, but he wasn't kissing her into accepting his marriage proposal. No way would she yield on that. Longing for him stabbed her, and she wanted to reach out and put her hand in his, but she couldn't.

Instead, she hugged her middle and slid out of the car when he held the door open for her. When she took her key out of her purse, his fingers closed over hers to take the key from her.

"Aaron, why don't we just say goodbye right here and right now? It would be so much more pleasant than arguing about our futures."

He unlocked the door, shoved it open and switched on the light. "Let's go inside," he said, stepping back.

"It won't do you any good," she stated, looking into his green eyes that blazed with determination. Taking a deep breath and knowing she was going into a contest of wills and a fierce verbal struggle, she moved past him into her apartment. Stunned, she halted.

With swiftly mounting horror she stared at overturned drawers, clothing, books and papers strewn everywhere, furniture slashed and stuffing pulled out. A scream worked its way up her throat as she gasped and clamped her hands over her mouth.

Five

Aaron pushed past her, already talking to someone about her apartment on his cellular phone. He switched his phone off. "The police are on their way over here."

He placed another call and she could hear him talking quietly, telling someone else about her place. When he shut off his phone and jammed it into his pocket, he motioned to her.

"You stay right here by the door while I look around," he said grimly.

He pulled a gun out of the waistband of his trousers at the small of his back, and she stared at it in horror. She knew nothing about guns and Aaron suddenly looked different carrying a weapon. Tall, rugged, dangerous. His green eyes were angry, and fear for his safety filled her until he glanced back at her and she looked into his eyes. His gaze held the coldness and hardness of ice, frightening her. She remembered him telling her about being in the military, and she realized now she was seeing a different, much tougher side to him.

She shivered, keeping her arms wrapped around herself. Who would do this to her? Why?

Aaron disappeared into her bedroom and the lights switched on. While she waited, she looked at the slashed pillows. Someone wanted something, but what? She had nothing of great value, nothing important to anyone except her.

In seconds Aaron returned minus the weapon. He crossed the room to her to pull her into his arms, and for the moment she was glad to feel the reassurance of his strong arms.

"Why, Aaron?"

"Somebody wants something they think you have," he replied grimly. "You're shivering."

"I feel violated to think some stranger has been in here, destroying my things. I don't have any valuables."

"You'll stay at my house tonight."

"I can stay at the hotel or with my friends."

"No, you can't." He leaned back. "You don't want to endanger your friends. You may be in danger. I want you to stay at my house," he declared in a tone that ended the discussion.

Nodding, she no longer wanted to argue with him. "I'm all right," she said, moving out of his arms. "I want to look at my things and see what's ruined."

"Wait until the law arrives. Let's not touch anything else because they may be able to get fingerprints." He pulled her close again and held her tightly, stroking her head.

They waited, and when he heard voices approaching, he took her arm and they went outside to meet two plainclothes detectives who introduced themselves as Ed Smith and Barney Whitlock.

"What time did y'all get here?" Detective Smith asked, and before she could answer, Aaron spoke up.

"About fifteen minutes ago. You made good time."

"We try."

While the men talked, Pamela listened in a daze, looking at her slashed and smashed belongings. Neighbors began to call, asking if she was all right, and if they could help. She talked on the phone constantly until Detective Whitlock wanted to take her statement. Aaron righted an overturned chair for her while the stocky, redheaded Whitlock stood nearby and wrote everything down on papers on a clipboard.

As she answered questions, all around her a police crew worked, moving in and out of the apartment, dusting for fingerprints, taking pictures, searching through the rubble. When Detective Whitlock finished with her statement and his questions, he lowered the clipboard.

"Thanks for your cooperation. We'll let you know anything we learn."

"Thank you," she said stiffly, wondering whether she would ever feel safe in her apartment again.

"Why don't you get what you want to take with you," Aaron suggested as soon as Whitlock moved away. "When they leave, the police will secure your place. They're leaving someone to watch your apartment."

"I didn't know they would do that." As soon as the words were spoken, she realized why they would guard her apartment. "You hired someone to watch my place, didn't you?"

"Yes. I want to. Don't worry about it because it's no big deal. He's an off-duty cop and glad for the extra work."

"Oh, Aaron!" she exclaimed, annoyed by his taking charge, yet glad, too, that someone would stand guard.

She walked cautiously to her bedroom, once more shaken by the destruction. Her mattress was flung on the floor. It was ripped and slashed, with the insides strewn about the room. Her clothes were tossed everywhere and to her dismay, when she looked at her dresses, most of them were slashed.

She fingered one and glanced around to find Aaron watching her from the doorway.

"What are they searching for, Aaron? What could anyone think I have that's valuable? I'm a teacher with no family. I don't have anything."

"Someone thinks you do," he answered grimly.

"I'll get what I can salvage." As she looked through her clothing, she thought about all the questions the Asterland investigators had asked her, and the many times they had asked about what jewels she carried. She studied Aaron while he stood waiting patiently. He looked relaxed as he leaned against the door, but she noticed he was methodically scrutinizing her room and she wondered what was running through his mind. Then her attention returned to gathering what she could to take with her to Aaron's.

Bits of lace underwear were tossed on the floor, and she felt violated again. Anger made her shake. "I hope they catch whoever did this."

"I'm just glad you weren't home," Aaron said quietly and turned away.

Pamela gathered a few clothes that were in one piece. She wanted to wash all of her clothing, as if by washing she could cleanse them of the stranger's invasive touch.

Twenty minutes later she and Aaron left her apartment. As they walked past the yellow police tape that cordoned off the area, she saw three of her teacher friends standing in a cluster.

"Aaron, come meet my friends."

After they hugged her, she introduced Aaron to Jan Raddison, Amy Barnes and Robin Stafford. While Aaron stood quietly waiting, they offered help and sympathy for her loss. When she said goodbye, she and Aaron walked only a few yards to find more friends waiting to talk to her. It was another thirty minutes before she was seated in Aaron's car to drive away.

"You have a lot of friends."

"They were nice to stand out there in the cold to see me. And their offers of help were gracious. If I wouldn't endanger one of them, I'd stay with them."

"This is better."

"Suppose I put you in danger?"

He glanced at her. "I'd like to catch whoever ransacked your apartment."

Realizing there was a side to him she didn't know and didn't want to know, she shivered and became silent. While they rode, her jangled nerves settled until they approached Pine Valley. As they drove through the gated entrance, she thought

of their first night in his house. Glancing at him, she wondered
if memories assailed him also. If so, he gave no indication.

Inside his house he dropped all her things in the utility room
except one small bag, and then he led her upstairs.

"Aaron, my robe was cut up."

"I'll give you one," he answered lightly. "I have a T-shirt
you can sleep in if you'd like."

"Yes. I want to wash everything before I wear it. I know
that's silly, but I feel as if everything I own fell into a mud
puddle. Or worse."

"I figured you'd want to wash your clothes." Halfway
down the hall to his large bedroom, he paused. "Being here
with you brings back memories," he said in a husky voice as
he brushed locks of hair away from her cheek.

"Yes, it does for me, too," she admitted. Their gazes
locked and held while tension filled the moment and the air
between them crackled.

"Which room will I stay in tonight?" she asked, prompting
him. A muscle worked in his jaw as he took her arm and
headed down the hall to the room next to his.

"I'll put you in here," he said. When he swung open the
door, she entered another huge bedroom with a queen-size
four-poster bed, a pale blue spread, thick cream-colored carpet
and mahogany furniture.

"This is lovely. Your home is beautiful."

"Thanks. Mom's the one to thank for that."

"Once again, I'm sorry you lost your parents," she said.

"I think that's why I was more than a little upset when I
heard about your plane having to make the forced landing."
He set down a small bag she had packed and turned to drape
his hands on her shoulders, kneading them lightly. She was
aware of his touch and of his searching gaze. She longed to
step closer and wrap her arms around him and feel his arms
around her.

"You were tense before the break-in. You're really uptight
now. Let's go downstairs and have some hot chocolate.
Okay?"

Nodding, she dropped her purse, and he helped her out of her coat and tossed it on a chair. He waited while she went out ahead of him.

In minutes they were seated in his family room in front of a roaring fire with cups of hot chocolate.

"Who do you think ransacked my apartment?" Pamela was curled in a corner of the sofa with her shoes off and her legs tucked under her. Aaron sat only inches away. He had shed his suit coat and tie and kicked off his shoes. His cup of chocolate sat on the table in front of them, and he reached out to twist her hair in his fingers. Each little touch sent tingles racing in her. Even though their conversation was impersonal and about her apartment, she was aware of how close he sat, of the fact that they would be under the same roof all night. Locks of his brown hair fell across his forehead, and while she watched, he unfastened two more buttons of his shirt. In the firelight that created an orange glow, he looked too appealing.

"I don't know. Whoever trashed your apartment will just know he didn't find what he was looking for. That doesn't mean you don't have it."

She shook her head angrily. "You were right, I suppose. I'm the one someone has been following."

"I chased someone from outside your apartment last night."

Shocked, she stared at him. "There was someone watching my apartment?" Goose bumps rose on her arms. "Why didn't you tell me?"

"I didn't want to worry you. I've cautioned you to be careful. I couldn't catch him. He went over a fence and jumped into a car and drove off. There were two of them."

"I'm glad you didn't catch him. Can't you leave that sort of thing for the police?"

He gave her a level look. "I wanted to catch him, and if I see him, I'll go after him again. I want to know why you're being followed."

She sipped her cocoa and set her cup down, all the while

studying him as she mulled over possibilities in her mind. Her curiosity rose as she pieced little things together.

"What's running through your mind?" he asked.

"You're in the Texas Cattleman's Club. I've heard rumors about the members doing things to help people in trouble. You're one of those members who help people, aren't you, Aaron?"

"When I need to be," he answered.

"You've known all along that I was the one being followed. How did you know that?"

He studied her. "It's all confidential, Pamela. Anything I tell you can't go any farther than between us."

"It won't."

"We're concerned that all of the women on the plane are in danger."

"Who is we?" she asked, mulling over what he was revealing and again feeling chilling surprise that she could be in danger.

"Justin Webb, Matt Walker, Ben Rassad, Dakota Lewis. You know some of them."

"If we're in danger, what's being done?"

"Matt is watching Lady Helena. Ben Rassad is going to watch Jamie Morris."

"And you're watching over me," she said, closing her eyes and wondering how she could get him out of her life. At the same time, she was glad he was there. She thought about the rumors she had heard about the members of the Texas Cattleman's Club, that they helped save deserving people, and she could imagine Aaron doing this. His diplomatic background would give him opportunity to help overseas; his wealth would give him freedom and resources. She remembered watching him move through her apartment with his gun in his hand.

"What's worrying you?"

She looked into his searching gaze. "What's worrying me is how you always can read my thoughts."

"Not really. If I could read your thoughts I wouldn't have asked what's worrying you. I would have known. But we do understand things about each other without having to say anything. Haven't you noticed?''

"I haven't noticed that I can guess your feelings. Not like you do with me."

"Maybe I'm concentrating more on you," he said quietly. "I'm fascinated with everything about you," he said softly, leaning forward to kiss her throat lightly.

"You just can't be. I'm so plain vanilla ordinary, West Texas born and bred," she said, barely aware of words, aware only of him.

"And I think that's absolutely wonderful. And, my lady, you need to remember I'm West Texas born and bred, too."

"It's been educated out of you. There's nothing about you that's countrified."

"My values are," he whispered.

As she pushed him gently away, she wondered if he could hear her pounding heart. When he stroked her throat, she realized he could feel her racing pulse beneath his fingers.

"I want you to stay with me until we catch them."

She rubbed her forehead. "Aaron, it'll complicate our lives more than ever."

"No, it won't. We don't even have to talk about pregnancy and babies and marriage if you don't want. Just stay here until it's safe to go home. Okay?"

She nodded, wondering how many nights that would take and how many nights she could stay out of his bed. "I'll stay if we won't talk about marriage."

His green eyes were dark as he tangled her hair in his fingers. "If that's what it takes to get you to stay, fine. No talk of marriage."

"Aaron, I told you that I've signed up to substitute teach. I don't want to do anything to jeopardize the safety of children. I can't imagine that I'm in danger, but then I'm shocked that someone searched my apartment."

"If you can afford to wait, it might be best if you didn' substitute for a little while. I don't think you would bring any element of danger into a classroom, but if you're a target maybe it's best not to take the chance. I don't think it'll be long before we learn something about what's going on. There are several of us working on it."

"You think all of us, Lady Helena and Jamie Morris, too, are in danger?"

"Yes," he repeated. "Just be alert to everything going on around you."

Once again she sat and studied him, piecing together questions and remembrances and what she knew about the Texas Cattleman's Club members.

"What's running through your mind now?" he asked, while his fingers continued to comb slowly through her hair and his other hand rested on her knee.

"Aaron, there's an old legend about Royal prospering because of jewels found in the War with Mexico. They were put away for safekeeping and, according to the legend, the town has prospered because of them. I always thought it was just a legend, a myth, and the jewels didn't actually exist. Now those investigators asked me so many questions, and I keep recalling a lot of questions from them about jewelry. Did I own any? What jewelry was I taking to Asterland? What valuables did I have? I told you the things they asked me."

"Yes, you did."

"Is the legend of the jewels true?"

He looked down at her knee, rubbing his fingers lightly over it.

"It's true," he said finally, meeting her gaze. "It's safer if most people think there's only a legend. Do you know any of the story about the jewels?"

"I've heard that old Tex Langley who founded the Texas Cattleman's Club hid the jewels that were found during the War with Mexico."

Aaron nodded, and more questions swirled in her mind, puzzle pieces that might explain some of the strange happenings lately.

"The Texas Cattleman's Club members are the sworn guardians of the jewels," Aaron said quietly. "I wasn't going to tell you about them because I thought the less you knew the safer you might be. Since you're getting more involved all the time, maybe you should be informed.''

"Those stones—are they safely hidden?''

She knew his answer before he gave a negative shake of his head.

"That's what they think I have? Good heavens! That's impossible.''

"Someone has one of the stones.''

"What are we talking about here? I'll keep it confidential, but is this why I've been followed?'' she asked, aghast that someone thought she had something highly valuable. "What are these stones? Are they valuable?''

"They're damn valuable. We've already recovered two of the jewels. Justin found the emerald and the harlequin opal on the Asterland jet. There's a missing red diamond.''

"I've never heard of red diamonds or harlequin opals,'' she said, growing more appalled that someone would think she possessed one of the stones.

"The black harlequin opal is the stone of justice. It's credited as a healing stone with the power to protect its owner not just from disease, but to give the owner wisdom. It's not as valuable as the emerald, which is two carats, but the opal holds a great deal of value because of its history.''

As Aaron talked, his fingers drifted across her nape, winding in her hair, sliding along her arm and then drawing circles on her knee. Every touch was fiery, causing a continual awareness and building the need that was already burning in her, taking half her attention from the problems at hand.

"I know that emeralds are sometimes considered healing stones,'' she said, barely thinking about the stones. "And I think I remember that an emerald was supposed to be the gemstone of Ceres, a Roman goddess.''

"The goddess of agriculture,'' he whispered, as he brushed a kiss on her cheek.

"They're the color of your eyes,'' she added, unable to

resist telling him. His gaze met hers, and the desire that flamed in the green depths curled her toes.

"I hope our baby has your blue eyes," he said in a husky voice and her body grew taut with desire while heat smoldered in her. "Beautiful blue eyes," he whispered, rubbing her cheek with his knuckles.

His words were magical, tempting and taunting, making her long for all she couldn't have. "When I think of my baby, I think of a green-eyed, brown-haired baby boy," she whispered, unable to keep her secrets to herself.

"Ahh, darlin'. When I think of *our* baby, I see a little blue-eyed, black-haired girl."

Her heart was squeezed as if a fist had closed around it, and she tried to close her mind to what he said before she lost control of her emotions.

"Aaron, we were talking about the jewels," she reminded him, catching her breath and knowing she sounded as disturbed as she felt. "The emerald—remember. What about the red diamond?" she asked, trying to concentrate on his words, but far more aware of his hand caressing her and the tempting magic of his words. As she caught his hand in hers, he watched her intently. "The red diamond," she prodded.

"Red diamonds are rare. They've been called the stone of kings. This particular one is over a carat with no flaws to the naked eye. Its value could be enormous now. These stones were stolen and taken on board the plane for Asterland."

"How do you know the red diamond was there, too?"

"It just is a logical conclusion. All three were stolen, two turn up on the plane—the third stone was bound to be there, but in the forced landing everything was tossed everywhere."

"Everything and everybody," she said. "That landing brought out the best and the worst in people. I'm sorry Lady Helena was hurt so badly. When we first boarded the plane, I talked to her a little. I didn't know the man who was hurt at all, but, from what I last heard, he's still in a coma."

"That's right. He's an Asterland cabinet member, Robert Klimt."

"Someone thinks I have a red diamond in my possession," she said, dismayed and realizing she might be in a great deal of danger. She ran her hand across her forehead. "I don't need this."

"Don't worry. You'll be safe here."

"I can't stay shut up in your house."

"You can for a few days. We're working on this."

"Then you're in even more danger. Someone may want something from me, but the person who's doing this may just want you and your friends out of the way. Aaron, be careful," she urged, while concern for his safety overrode all her other stormy emotions.

"You *care,* darlin', a lot more than you want to admit," he said in a husky voice. His eyes darkened, and his gaze lowered to her mouth. Every inch of her flesh tingled, her lips parting because she couldn't get her breath. Her breasts were taut, and the heat smoldering so low inside her became a wildfire that raced along her veins. He was ruggedly handsome, too appealing, too irresistible. And the way he was looking at her now made her tremble. Forbidden, tantalizing, he was all she wanted.

Unable to resist, she leaned toward him and closed her eyes.

His mouth covered hers, his tongue sliding over her lower lip, touching the tip of her tongue and then stroking it while he lifted her onto his lap.

Throwing caution to the wind, she slid her arm around his neck, feeling his heart pounding in his chest as she placed her other hand against him. She twisted free his buttons and rested her hand on his solid chest. His heart thudded just as hers did. She let her hand drift lower to his flat stomach and she heard him growl deep in his throat. He was aroused, constrained by the suit trousers. She longed to just let go completely, to follow her heart and yield and love him. She did love him and she had to hold back the words because if she said them, he would, too, and his would be meaningless.

He leaned over her, shifting so she was lying on the sofa. While he kissed her, his hand slipped beneath her dress and he pulled away her panty hose, his fingers caressing her warm, bare thigh.

She wanted to spread her legs and arch her back and let him love her. Everything in her cried out for him, her body, her heart. Instead, she pushed against his chest.

Pausing, he raised his head. His green eyes were stormy and filled with scalding desire as he stared at her. "I love you," he said.

She placed her fingers on his mouth. "Shh. Stop that, Aaron." Hurting and wanting him, wanting his love and wishing he meant it, but keeping a grip on reality, she sat up and then stood.

"I should go to bed. Alone."

His darkened emerald eyes conveyed his roiling emotions. She was buffeted by his will, yet she knew the time would come when he would look at all this in a more rational manner, and be glad he wasn't married to her out of duty. He was aroused, his belt unbuckled, his shirt pushed open to reveal his muscular chest, covered in a mat of chest hair. Locks of straight brown hair fell across his forehead and his mouth was red from her kisses. He looked incredibly appealing and she found it wrenching to turn and walk away from him.

If only...

She knew better than to follow that line of thinking, but it was so difficult to resist. *If only he really did love her. If only they had known each other under different circumstances.*

Oh, sure, a small voice whispered in her mind. It wouldn't have mattered how different the circumstances. She was still small-town West Texas and he was jet-set, international man of the world. It wouldn't have mattered what circumstances. She could not link her life to his any easier than a Texas filly could link its life to a shooting star.

Picking up her discarded panty hose, she went upstairs, pausing at the top of the steps. He hadn't followed her, but had let her go.

"I love you."

His words rang in her ears, and he had sounded convincing.

She hurt so badly with wanting him. With wanting it *all*—his love, their marriage, their baby. Aaron, a father, there all the time for their child. Hurting, she clutched her middle and hurried to her bedroom, closing the door and leaning against it, feeling drained of all energy. Feeling drained of hope. She placed her hand against her stomach. She had his baby. She would always have that part of him. Tears stung her eyes, and she wiped at them furiously and moved to the bed where he had placed a large T-shirt of his and a navy velvet robe.

Gathering up the T-shirt and robe, she went to the adjoining bathroom, showered and pulled on the T-shirt, too aware that it was his. She slipped into the soft, elegant robe that was fancier than anything she had ever owned. She heard a knock, and her pulse jumped as she stared at the door.

Feeling a mixture of trepidation and eagerness, she crossed the room and opened the door.

Aaron stood there with his hands on his hips. He had shed his shirt and his trousers rode low on his narrow hips. His gaze was as stormy as ever as it swept slowly over her.

"Do you look good!" he said in a husky voice. He looked into her eyes, studying her.

"Did you want something, Aaron?"

His brow arched. "You," he said, his voice dropping still lower, and her heart thudded.

"We're not—"

"I know we're not, but I wanted to kiss you good-night."

"Oh, Aaron!" Against all good sense, she stepped forward and moved into his arms. In a deft movement that she never even noticed, he had the robe unbelted and pushed open, his arm sliding around her waist as he pulled her tightly against him and leaned over her to kiss her for all he was worth.

Aaron's pulse pounded hot and heavy as her soft curves pressed against him. Only his T-shirt covered her, and he longed to shove it away and caress her. He slid his hand beneath the shirt, running his fingers over the luscious smooth curve of her bottom, feeling her move against him. And then

NO POSTAGE
NECESSARY
IF MAILED
IN THE
UNITED STATES

BUSINESS REPLY MAIL

FIRST-CLASS MAIL   PERMIT NO. 717   BUFFALO, NY

POSTAGE WILL BE PAID BY ADDRESSEE

SILHOUETTE READER SERVICE

3010 WALDEN AVE

PO BOX 1867

BUFFALO NY 14240-9952

GET FREE BOOKS
and a
FREE GIFT WHEN YOU PLAY THE...

*Just scratch off the gold box
with a coin. Then check
below to see the gifts you get!*

YES!

I have scratched off the gold Box. Please send me my
2 FREE BOOKS and **gift for which I qualify.** I understand
that I am under no obligation to purchase any books
as explained on the back of this card.

326 SDL C6Q7

225 SDL C6Q3
(S-D-OS-02/01)

NAME	(PLEASE PRINT CLEARLY)
ADDRESS	
APT.#	CITY
STATE/PROV.	ZIP/POSTAL CODE

7	7	7	Worth TWO FREE BOOKS plus a BONUS Mystery Gift!
🍒	🍒	🍒	Worth TWO FREE BOOKS!
🔔	🔔	♣	TRY AGAIN!

Offer limited to one per household and not valid to current Silhouette
Desire® subscribers. All orders subject to approval.

his hand went up to the small of her back, caressing, memorizing her.

When she pushed against him, he released her reluctantly. Stepping back, she stared at him with huge blue eyes that danced with searing flames. Her breathing was as harsh and fast as if she had run a mile. Her mouth was pouty and red from their kisses. And the T-shirt clung, revealing the taut peaks of her nipples.

He wanted her and he loved her. And she only believed half the truth.

"Good night, Aaron," she said. She closed the door, and he stared at it, wanting to kick it open and take her in his arms and kiss her until he melted every protest.

Instead, Aaron returned to his room and took a cold shower that did nothing to cool him down. As the cold spray hit him, he shifted his thoughts to her apartment. Not a cushion had been left untouched. Her wicker furniture had been ripped apart, and all her dresses had been slashed. Someone had to be searching for the missing red diamond. The Texas Cattleman's Club members didn't have it, but then, neither did someone else who had to have known it was on the Asterland jet.

This made Jamie Morris and Lady Helena incredibly vulnerable, too, but Ben and Matt would protect them.

Who had the diamond? What had happened to it in the forced landing? And the jewels had to be tied to Asterland for the two Asterland investigators to question Pamela so much about what jewelry she was carrying. The jewels were priceless, so a fortune could be gained from their possession. But because of his background, he couldn't keep from thinking of other possibilities for the money from the sale of the stones. Terrorism? Revolution? Drugs? Weapons? They had to find the missing diamond and all clues seemed to indicate that it was still somewhere in Royal. Someone thought it was in Pamela's possession.

He turned off the shower and toweled dry, climbing into

bed to stare into the darkness. He was aroused, taut and aching for her. Aware she was only yards away. He went over the entire day, the news of her pregnancy, their arguments, their date.

He searched his own feelings for her. Was it sex as she accused? He tried to study his feelings impartially, tried to sort out what he felt from what his body desired. And the more he thought about it and considered and remembered, the more he determined that he was deeply, irrevocably in love with his West Texas lady.

"Lady, I love you," he whispered into the darkness, turning to look at the door and thinking about her in the next bedroom.

He did love her. The more he searched his feelings, the more certain he became. He was head over heels, unable to get her out of his thoughts, heart-pounding in love with her. She filled this great aching emptiness in him that had grown worse the past couple of years. When he was around her, his life had purpose. Even now, with all the disagreements and turmoil between them, he didn't have that chilling desolation that filled him most of the time in the recent past. And she was so much that he admired—good with children, intelligent, sexy, caring, fun.

She would have to come to realize the depth of his feelings for her. He thought about five years from now, ten years—and he knew if it was five or a lifetime, she was truly the woman for him.

"I really love you with a love that's bigger than Texas, and, whether you let me show you or not, my love will last," he said in the darkness, and his resolve to convince her of his feelings grew.

Their first and only night together, he had taken her virginity and gotten her pregnant. From what all his friends had told him about her, she had never really dated anyone. Which meant she had never really been courted by anyone. She deserved that much. He sat up, thinking about what he could do and mapping out his plans just as he had mapped out every important move in his life.

He switched on a light and moved to his desk to jot down things he wanted to do first thing in the morning. When he was back in bed in the dark, he mulled over everything that had happened and he looked again at the closed bedroom door, thinking about her so near and yet so impossibly far. "You're my lady, and I'm not letting you and our baby go out of my life. I love you, Pamela," he said, and searched his own feelings. Would he feel the same if there were no baby?

He realized that that was the critical question. He had to get all thoughts of their baby out of his mind and look at his emotions and feelings. For the next half hour he lay in the dark, mulling over every moment with her, all his feelings, his longings. What would he feel if she wasn't pregnant?

His conclusion was the same. The more he was around her, the more he was certain he truly loved her, and the more he wanted her. No woman had ever had that effect on him. And first thing in the morning he would try to show her every way possible how much she meant to him.

He slept little and was up so early, he dressed in sweats and jogged, circling his block for half an hour so he would never be far from the house and watching to see if he could spot anyone lurking in the area. He returned, showered, dressed in jeans and a wool shirt and saw that her bedroom door was still closed. He paused beside it and didn't hear a sound, so guessed she was sleeping. Taunting images of silky long legs and luscious curves floated in his mind and, without thinking, his hand closed around the doorknob. Reluctantly, he released the knob, turned and went downstairs to start breakfast, wondering what she could eat that wouldn't cause morning sickness. It was still early, but his housekeeper usually arrived at half-past six, so he called her and made arrangements for her to come only once a week. He called the family cook with the same instructions. He wanted Pamela to himself as much as possible.

The moment the clock struck half-past seven he called the local florist at home. Since the turn of the century, the Hanleys had been in the flower business in Royal, and Aaron had gone to school with Rufus Handley who ran the Handley Floral Shop now. In minutes he had ordered three dozen red roses to be delivered today.

Impatiently, he waited until eight and then made more calls while he moved around the kitchen finishing breakfast preparations.

"Good morning," Pamela said.

He turned and his insides clenched. She wore his robe and was barefoot, her skin glowing and her hair still damp. He dropped whatever he was holding, unaware of what he was doing except moving toward her. He couldn't resist going to her. He had to touch and hold her and he knew he was absolutely, irrevocably in love with her.

Six

Immobilized by the intensity of his gaze, Pamela could barely catch her breath and every thought flew out of her mind. He narrowed the space between them and a thrill curled down through her to the center of her being. There was no question he desired her, but there was a quality of something else in his expression—tenderness? Love?

It couldn't be, she reminded herself, but her pulse raced as he closed the distance and his arm went around her to pull her against him.

"Oh, Aaron, don't do this to us. It—"

There were no more words because his mouth covered hers, and he kissed her long and deep with a soul-searching passion. His hands moved beneath the robe and T-shirt until she caught his wrists and leaned away.

"Aaron, don't keep doing this to us!" she pleaded again, gasping for breath, trying to do what she knew she should do.

"I love you."

"Shh. Stop saying words you didn't say until you knew you should marry me!"

He framed her face with his hands. "I love you and I won't stop saying it because it's true. I was awake hours last night, and I searched my feelings."

"Stop saying things you don't really mean, or I'm moving out of your house. I have a friend in Midland and—"

"I'll stop," he interrupted grimly. "You stay right here at my house where it's safe."

She caught a whiff of an acrid smell. Smoke curled over the burners and a dreadful smell assaulted her, sending her stomach rolling.

"Something's burning!" As her stomach heaved, she fled. She heard swearing behind her and a clatter of utensils. She hoped he hadn't set his house on fire, but she had to run for the bathroom.

Nauseated, embarrassed again, and unable to stop thinking about the past few moments, she rushed to a downstairs bathroom. After her stomach stopped heaving, she took a clean washcloth from the linen cabinet and sponged her face with cold water.

No man had ever looked at her the way Aaron had. Just the memory heated her and took her breath. In agony, she closed her eyes and placed her fist against her heart. Why was he making this so difficult!

"Get out of his house," she told herself, but then she remembered her trashed apartment and knew she couldn't go back to it. Her stomach settled, and she belted her robe and went back to the kitchen, promising herself that she would resist him. Embarrassed by her morning sickness, she entered the kitchen cautiously. The smells had gone; a fan whirred softly above the burners, and Aaron had his back to her as he reached into the refrigerator.

Watching him, she looked at his thick brown hair, her gaze drifting down across his broad shoulders, sliding lower to his narrow waist and slim hips. He wore faded jeans and once again looked like a lot of local cowboys except that he was

Aaron. There was no way she could ever look at him and see Aaron as an ordinary man. Not once, not from that first moment of looking into his eyes across the Texas Cattleman's Club ballroom, had she ever been able to view him with the same objective manner she did all other men. And she knew she never would.

As if he sensed she was there, he turned. He held a pitcher of orange juice and he studied her. "All right now?" he asked gently.

"Yes. You're very nice about my morning sickness. I'd think it would send most guys running."

He shoved the refrigerator door shut and shrugged. "I grew up on a ranch and you see a lot of things. Birth, death, mating, fighting—it's all there and it's part of living. Sure you're all right now?"

"I'm fine. Did you burn something?"

"Yes, but fortunately, it was contained in a skillet. I tried to get all of the smells out of the room. Now, what can you eat?"

"Actually, that orange juice looks good. Sometimes this hits and then it passes and then other times, I can't eat anything until afternoon. And sometimes food looks so good, I eat and then I lose it."

"Come sit down and try out my cooking," he said, smiling with a flash of white teeth, and once again becoming his irresistible, irrepressible self.

The round oak table was set and looked inviting with cheerful bright blue place mats and colorful china. She took a tentative sip of her orange juice, aware of Aaron seated across the table from her and watching her with a faint smile.

"What do you have to do today?" he asked.

"I have an appointment with the obstetrician. I told his nurse about my morning sickness, but I don't think he can do much for it. My appointment is at eleven. Then I'll go to my apartment and see what I can do there."

Aaron shook his head. "I'll take you to the doctor's, and then we can have lunch together. I hired a cleaning crew to work on your apartment as soon as the police will let anyone go back inside.''

She lowered the glass of cold juice to the table and memories swirled in her mind of gifts men showered on her mother and her and how much she had hated having to accept them.

''Aaron, I don't want you to hire someone to clean my apartment. You don't have to do things like that for me.'' She knew she was overreacting, but she was too conscious of being pregnant and unwed, too conscious of Dr. Woodbury's reaction that lumped her together with her mother. ''I don't want you to do that for me,'' she snapped.

His smile vanished and he studied her, reaching across the table to take her hand. She tried to pull away, but he held her firmly.

''What is it?'' he asked. ''You're not giving me a polite 'oh, you shouldn't have' objection. I've upset you, but why? What is it?''

''I can take care of myself,'' she said stiffly, withdrawing her hand from his.

With a scrape, he pushed back his chair and came around the table. She watched him as he paused beside her and held out his hand. ''Come here.''

''Aaron, we'll end up in each other's arms and at a stalemate.''

''I just want to talk. I think we need to talk because I don't understand why you're upset.''

When she stood, he picked her up, sitting in her chair and holding her on his lap. Her heart raced as she looked into his eyes. She was only inches from him and could smell his aftershave, see his clean-shaven jaw that was smooth and tan. His lashes were unbelievably thick and gave him sexy, bedroom eyes that were irresistible.

''I don't think this is a good way to have a reasonable discussion,'' she said, barely able to get her breath, too conscious of him to think straight.

''I think it's the best way,'' he said easily as if they were in an office and seated across the room from each other. He seemed undisturbed by her closeness until she looked into his eyes, and the longing she saw there was unmistakable. "My hiring help for you really disturbs you. Why?"

"I can take care of my apartment. I'm used to taking care of myself. I took care of my mother all the last years of her life and I was only in high school. I don't want you doing things like that for me."

Aaron pushed locks of her hair away from her face, tucking them behind her ear and letting his fingers trail over her ear. "I want to do things like that for you. Please let me."

She shook her head, not trusting her voice to speak. She thought of how much like her mother she had been, tumbling into bed with Aaron the first night she met him.

"Mellie," he said softly. "That's a good nickname. I'll commandeer that from the little girls. What's bothering you?"

"Nothing," she replied stiffly, aware when he drawled the nickname it sounded infinitely more personal than when it was said by the children.

"Good, then you'll let me do these things for you."

"No, I won't!" she answered fiercely. "I'll be just like my mother, sleeping with someone and then taking gifts—" She bit her lip and looked away.

"Ahh, here's what's disturbing you," he said so gently her insides wrenched. "You're not like your mother. No one could possibly think that."

"Yes, they could. Dr. Woodbury did the moment he found out I was pregnant."

"Then I'm damn glad you have another doctor," Aaron said, his green eyes turning cold. "And it might have been your imagination. Darlin', I've talked to guys I know here. Your reputation is impeccable."

"When they find out that I'm pregnant, they'll just see my mother in me. That sterling reputation will be tarnished forever," She locked her fingers together in her lap while painful memories taunted her. "Aaron, the men that came to our house…they would bring presents to her. They gave her all kinds of gifts. And they brought gifts to me to try to please her, and when I was small, she made me accept them." She met his gaze and couldn't keep the anguish out of her voice, while hating herself for spilling so much of what she had always kept hidden. "That's where I got money for my clothes. That's how we got our furniture. That's where she got her cars. Kids would tell me she was the town tramp, and they were right. But now that's all people will think of when my pregnancy shows." As old hurts welled up in her, her throat burned while she struggled with her emotions. "The first time you looked at me, I just fell into your arms and into your bed. Everyone will compare me to her and say I'm like her. I don't want your gifts!"

She started to get up, but his arms wrapped around her and he held her. "No, they won't," he answered firmly.

"Let me go, Aaron. I've lived with this. I've lived with them calling my mother all kinds of ugly names and calling me trash and such."

"That was a long time ago. You haven't heard anyone call you a name since you've grown up, have you?"

She didn't want to look at him. Embarrassment flooded her and she just wanted to be gone, out of his scrutiny, out of temptation, back to the security of her quiet life.

He put his finger beneath her chin and turned her to face him. "That was a long time ago and I'm not giving you gifts in payment for sex. I'm doing the things I want to do for my lady, the love of my heart."

"Aaron, stop it. If I married you, you know what your family would think. They'd think I trapped you into it." She wiped furiously at tears that brimmed over and spilled down her cheeks. "I can't control anything with you. Too many times now you've seen me at my worst."

"And the worst looks pretty damn good to me," he said quietly, giving another wrench to her heart.

"Stop being so adorable!" she cried, wriggling to get off his lap.

His arms tightened, holding her against him. "I want to do things for you, and wanting to doesn't have anything to do with that night. Now let me. Guys all over the world do things they want to do for women in their lives. Let me do what I want for you. And I want you always to know that it's because I love you and not because we went to bed together."

"I don't believe it."

"Just give me a chance here. We haven't had sex since that first night. If having sex was why I want to shower you with things, do you think I'd continue? Of course, I wouldn't."

"Aaron, the smooth-talking diplomat in you is showing," she said, knowing she was going to give in, yet suddenly feeling better. "Everyone will think I'm like her."

"No, they won't. For them to think bad things about you, there will have to be *men* in your life. Not just one particular man who wants to marry you. Believe me, you have a reputation for being very cool and collected." He stroked her face lightly with his fingers and his voice was so tender, she knew some of her hurts were vanishing.

"Maybe I'm too sensitive about it, but I've spent most of my life struggling with insults and men making passes and being ostracized."

"Oh, damn, darlin', I wish I could take away the hurt, but that was a long time ago and it has nothing to do with us."

"I can't turn hurts from my past off, Aaron."

"I know you can't. But what I feel and do has nothing to do with what happened when you were growing up." He stroked her head, running his fingers through her hair while he held her close. Touching the strong column of his throat, still aware of his arm holding her tightly, she took his hand to hold it in hers.

"I've never told anyone all that."

"I'm glad you told me. I've never told anyone how purposeless my life has become the past few years. But the desolation is gone when I'm with you."

She searched his thickly lashed green eyes, and he met her gaze squarely. "When I think about your lifestyle," she whispered, "I just can't believe you don't have everything you could possibly want. And I can't believe I give meaning to your life.''

"I'll show you, lady. This is one Texan who knows what he wants, and I'm going to try to make it clear to you just how deep my feelings run. They're bigger than Texas, stronger than the Texas wind, as lasting as that hard-packed West Texas ground. I love you, Pamela Miles, and that's the only reason for the gifts from me.''

Golden and warm, his words washed over her, melting away her hurts, and she wanted to believe them. For the moment she did. She couldn't resist him.

"You sweet-talkin' charmer,'' she whispered, and wound her arms around his neck, and knew he had won another round as she leaned forward to place her lips on his. She saw the one second of surprise that widened his eyes, and then his arm tightened around her, and he leaned over her to kiss her. His hand stroked her back and he wound his fingers through her hair, kissing her until she was gasping for breath and her hands were all over him. He was aroused; there was no mistaking he wanted her. And she wanted him, but she knew she shouldn't.

Aaron was the one who raised his head and shifted her away. "I want you.'' He ground out the words in a husky voice. "And you're going to be mine, but it isn't because of sex that I want to do things for you.'' He scooted her off his lap.

Standing, she pulled her robe together and realized he had stopped kissing her to try to prove to her his feelings weren't driven by sex. She suffered another twist to her heart.

Her body throbbed with need, her breasts were taut and tingled and she wanted to sit back in his lap and kiss him, but this was best. And there was no mistaking that he wanted her. He was aroused, ready. His forehead was beaded with sweat and the hunger in his eyes made her knees jelly.

"I can't eat any breakfast,'' she whispered. "I'll get ready for my doctor's appointment.''

"Pamela.''

At the door she turned as he stood. "I need to go to a meeting. I'll come back in time to take you to the doctor."

She nodded and went upstairs, mulling over all the things they had said to each other.

In spite of his arguments, she was reluctant to accept the cleaning service. It seemed ridiculous when she wasn't working, and she couldn't shake the old feelings that she was doing what her mother had done and would bring down the same reaction from townspeople. It was just a matter of time before her pregnancy was known, and then the gossip would start. If people knew she was living in Aaron's Pine Valley home, gossip would start even sooner.

After showering and dressing, Pamela meandered through Aaron's elegant mansion, looking at family pictures, studying pictures of his brothers and his sister. They all had brown hair. A brother and his sister had green eyes, the other brother, the minister, had blue eyes.

Dr. Rebecca Black. Pamela had heard about his sister's work in remote areas of the world, now in the jungles of Belize. In this picture, Aaron's sister had short brown hair and looked practical and intelligent and, judging from childhood pictures, had been a tomboy.

Pamela studied the two brothers' pictures, Jeb Black managed the family fortune and lived in Houston. "He's our hard-headed businessman," Aaron had said, describing his family.

The other brother, the minister, was shorter than the rest of the men in his family. He was Reverend Jacob Black whose reputation was international because of the money he raised and channeled into church missionary work around the world.

With his rugged features, his height and his slender build, Aaron resembled his dad.

The doorbell rang and Pamela went to a window. Before he'd left, Aaron had told her not to answer the door unless she knew for certain who it was, which had made her laugh.

"Who knows I'm staying here?" she questioned, amused by his instructions. She'd stood at the back door with him while he pulled on a shearling coat and picked up a black Stetson.

"You might be surprised, darlin'," he drawled in his West Texas accent, touching her cheek. "I like your dimples, Mellie. If someone comes to the door, before you open it, just make sure you know who it is. Now set the alarm when I close the door."

"Sure thing, cowboy," she said with a wink, and he drew a deep breath, coming back in to haul her into his arms and kiss her senseless. When he released her, he looked down at her solemnly. "You're going to be mine, Mellie," he whispered. Then he had jammed his hat down farther on his head, turned and left while she stood breathlessly watching him.

As the soft melodic chimes rang again, she came out of her reverie and experienced a swift stab of apprehension when the sight of her trashed apartment flashed in mind. Concerned, she hurried to an upstairs window and looked down at the drive. At first glance she recognized the robin's-egg-blue van with bright yellow letters, Handley's Floral Shop. With relief surging in her, she hurried downstairs to the door.

When she looked through a peephole, she recognized Rufus Handley's brown eyes and blond hair above an enormous bouquet of red roses.

"Oh, my!" She stared at the flowers in surprise and then jumped when Rufus punched the doorbell again. She turned off the alarm, unlocked and opened the door.

"Hi, Miss Miles," he said with a wide smile. She had had his little girl in her second-grade class three years ago. "I have some flowers for you."

"For me?" she asked, feeling embarrassed, amazed and chagrined all at once.

"Can I bring them inside?"

"Of course," she said, stepping back and looking at the enormous bouquet of gorgeous red roses. "How's Trisha?"

"She's great. You can't believe how well she's reading. Ms. Stafford said she's two levels beyond her grade."

"That's great!"

"Well, we owe a lot to you. You really helped her with her reading."

"She's a very bright girl and a very sweet one."

He grinned. "I'll tell Lucy and Trisha you said that. Enjoy your flowers. I'm sorry your apartment was broken into. We don't have much of that around here, so I hope they catch who did it soon. You've had some bad luck lately, with the plane going down and now having a break-in. I'm sorry."

"Thanks," she said, following him to the door and closing it behind him, knowing Royal was small enough that people still knew most everything that was happening in town. She reset the alarm and then walked back to the bouquet, laughing and shaking her head. The roses were beautiful. She pulled out the card.

To Pamela With Love. Aaron.

"Oh, no!" She let the card flutter from her hand and fall to the floor and her amusement and joy over the flowers vanished. By nightfall it would be all over Royal that she was staying at Aaron's house and he had sent her roses and signed the card "with love, Aaron."

"Oh, no!" she whispered again, embarrassment flooding her. He might as well have put banner headlines in the newspaper.

"Why did you sign it that way?" she asked the empty house. Even though she was home alone, her cheeks flushed with embarrassment. Rufus Handley and everyone at his shop would know about the card and flowers, and before long the whole town would know. Why hadn't Aaron just signed his name and let it go at that?

Her embarrassment was tinged with anger. Aaron Black had a streak of bulldog stubbornness.

He was picking her up to take her to her doctor's appointment, but she didn't want to see him or go to the obstetrician with him and add to the rumors about them that would already be flying. The sight of Aaron Black escorting her into the obstetrician's office would be more noticeable than banners waving over the town. Heavens, what talk that would start!

She should have told him no when he offered to take her to the doctor's office, but when she was with him, her thoughts were always half jumbled.

Hurrying to the phone, she called the only cab that served Royal, knowing that would be just one more rumor because she had been picked up at Aaron's house on another occasion—near dawn that first morning.

She locked up and left, going to her doctor's appointment early and calming as they discussed her morning sickness.

When she stepped out of Dr. Burke's office, Aaron was lounging against the wall in the hallway. His hat was pushed back on his head. Sunglasses were hooked into a pocket of his shirt. He had shed his coat and held it in one hand. At the sight of her, he straightened. "I thought I was going to pick you up and bring you here for your appointment."

"The flowers are beautiful."

"And another gift is worrying you. I thought we settled that this morning."

"Aaron, you signed the card 'with love.' I'm staying at your house. Pretty soon it'll be all over town. And if you had escorted me here—to the obstetrician's—what talk that would stir!"

Dropping his coat, he turned her so she was against the wall and he braced both hands on either side of her, hemming her in. He glanced around them at the empty hallway. "Look, lady. You have the most exemplary reputation in town. I know you have old hurts and I'm sorry."

"This isn't about that," she whispered, surprised by the forcefulness of his words. "It's that everyone—" She faltered over the words. "Everyone will think—"

"Will think I'm in love. That's fine and dandy. I could shout it from the rooftops because I am and there's nothing to be ashamed of or to hide about it. I love you, Pamela," he announced clearly.

"Aaron, don't!" she cried, hurting. "You don't know what you feel and you didn't say that to me until you thought we had to get married."

Aaron glanced over his shoulder again. Following his gaze, she glanced down the empty hallway as a door closed at the end of the hall.

He took her arm. "Let's talk somewhere else," he said tersely.

She walked with him out to his car. Wind buffeted her while he unlocked the car door, and she watched him look around. "You think I'm being followed again."

"Yes, I do. While we were talking, someone was at the end of the hall. I would have gone after them, but that would have left you there alone and that's not good."

She shivered and sat down in his car, watching him go around to the driver's side. He slid in and looked at her. "Marry me and we'll stop all worry about gossip."

"No. We've been over this. And you said you wouldn't talk about marriage while I'm at your house."

"We're not at my house now. I love you and I could happily spread it on billboards or in the newspaper or anywhere else."

"Don't!"

"I'm not going to because it wouldn't make you happy," he said solemnly. "But I am going to keep right on trying to get you to face the truth about yourself and about me." He stroked her cheek lightly with his fingers. "Darlin', you're getting over old hurts and I know that takes time. I can be patient because it's important."

She inhaled deeply, looking into the depths of his direct gaze and feeling that he meant every word now. Yet she was still certain he would change in time.

"What did the doctor say?" Aaron asked while his eyes conveyed a hungry intensity that made her think his mind was barely on his words.

"He said I should try to eat when I can. I've lost some weight," she said, aware of Aaron, knowing someone outside had followed her again and she should be more concerned about the danger she might be in, but all she could think about was Aaron and his declarations of love that had sounded absolute. If only she could believe him. If only, if only…

She realized he was staring at her intently. "I'm sorry. Did you say something?"

"I said a lot. What're you thinking about?"

"What you've said to me in the past few minutes."

"Good! I want you to think about what I'm telling you because every word I've said is true. Sooner or later you're going to see that I mean what I say."

"I still don't think you're giving this enough serious thought."

"Did the doc give you anything for the morning sickness?"

"No. He said that will pass after the third month—"

"That's a long time."

"It'll go in a hurry."

"Can you eat lunch now?"

"Yes, as a matter of fact, I feel starved."

"Is the Royal Diner okay?"

"Sure."

She noticed he still watched the rearview mirror as he drove. Main Street had the ordinary amount of traffic, the usual number of people walking in front of buildings, going in and out of stores, but someone out there had ransacked her apartment and slashed her belongings. Someone out there had followed her to her doctor's appointment. Someone out there thought she had a rare red diamond worth heaven knows how much. The idea chilled her.

"Aaron, where can that diamond be? Are you sure it isn't still at the landing site and all of your friends overlooked it?"

He shook his head. "That site has been searched inch by inch, by not only Texas Cattleman's Club members, but investigators and lawmen. No, it's somewhere else, and we're not the only ones searching for it."

"Why would anyone think I had it?"

"Why *not* you, darlin'?" he drawled. "You'd be the perfect cover, particularly if you didn't know you were carrying it."

"If I'd had it in my belongings, I would know it now because I unpacked everything."

"You're sure?"

"Very sure. And the clothing I took with me on the plane was in the apartment, so it's been slashed and pawed over." She bit her lip. "Whoever is searching for the diamond has to know now that I don't have it."

"Not necessarily. Someone followed you to the doctor's."

"So someone is watching your house," she said, and saw a muscle working in his jaw.

"We'll catch whoever it is."

"I don't find that reassuring. Please be careful."

He turned to give her a quick searching look and then looked at the street as he slowed for a stoplight. After parking in front of the diner, Aaron took her arm and they hurried inside.

Over hamburgers that tasted delicious to her and a thick creamy chocolate malt, she listened to Aaron talk about his life in Spain. Long after they finished, they still sat and talked until he glanced at his watch. "I have an appointment with our local attorney at four. I'll take you home unless you have somewhere else you want to go."

"Your house is fine," she said, reluctant to go to her apartment if she didn't have to.

"Good. Will it bother you to fly?"

"I don't think so, but I don't plan on any trips soon."

"How about dinner tonight in Dallas with me?"

She closed her eyes. "Aaron, you're not getting what I'm telling you."

"Yes, I am. I told you, I want to show you that you're important to me and I'm in love." He slid out of the booth and stood waiting, holding her coat for her when she stood. He draped his arm over her shoulders and she knew that everyone in Royal would be linking them together now.

Monday morning he took her back to look at her apartment. Aaron unlocked the door and put his arm around her as they entered. "I'm having an alarm installed this morning."

She turned to stare at him, but before she could speak, he put his finger on her lips. "Shh. I'm doing what I want to do. You need an alarm, and I know you hadn't even thought about getting one, had you?"

"No. I don't know that I'll continue living in Royal."

A fleeting look of pain flashed in his eyes and was gone. "All right, so it's temporary," he said grimly. "At least, for now, humor me and accept my present."

She studied him and could feel the clash of wills, yet knew his intentions had been good. "Thank you," she said, and he leaned forward to brush a kiss on her forehead.

"You're welcome. The guy should be out here in thirty minutes to install it. Insurance will cover your losses on your furniture and clothing."

"Please, Aaron, don't replace my furniture," she said solemnly.

He studied her and held her shoulders, rubbing them lightly. "I'm just trying to do things to help, not hurt."

"I know you are and the flowers are beautiful and the alarm will be very nice, but I'm accustomed to taking care of myself. Besides, I want to pick out my own furniture."

"You don't like the way my house looks?" he teased, trying to lighten the moment.

"Your mother did your house, not you. You leave my furniture to me."

"Fine, but let me at least buy you a new dress and take you out in it."

She smiled and shook her head. "I think you're incredibly used to getting your own way."

"Might be a little, but I think you are, too."

"Not like you are, Aaron," she remarked dryly, thinking of his unlimited funds that allowed him to do so much of what he wanted.

"Maybe that's what makes me so lovable."

She had to laugh then. "That and your modesty."

He grinned, touching her dimple. "If you only knew what

your smiles do for me. They chase away all my rainy days. Come on, let's see how things look."

When they entered her living room, she drew a deep breath. The cleaning service had the floors polished and things righted. The room smelled of lemon furniture polish and surfaces gleamed. Books were on bookshelves, but most tables and shelves were bare because her vases and candlesticks had been broken. Throw cushions were gone; her pictures were stacked on the floor against a wall, the frames broken, the glass that had covered them gone or cracked. The few pieces of furniture that were not ruined were in place, but the cushions had slashes in them and the apartment was not livable. She went to the kitchen and found some of her dishes and utensils intact, but most crystal was gone and much of her china, swept out of cabinets carelessly to the floor when the intruder had searched her apartment.

"I hope you do catch who did this," she said quietly.

The cleaning service had hauled away the ripped mattress and springs, so she had only a frame for a bed. Loss overwhelmed her and she ran her fingers across her brow.

"They're only things, Mellie," Aaron said gently, pulling her closer against his side. "You're safe and that's what's important. This can all be replaced."

"I know—" The doorbell rang, startling her, and she realized how tense she was. "That's probably the girls," she said, turning to answer. He caught her arm.

"Let me go to the door," he said grimly, moving ahead of her.

Seven

She moved cautiously behind Aaron. As he paused to look through the new peephole, he motioned to her to join him. When he opened the door and stepped back, Pamela faced her next-door neighbor who stood holding a casserole.

"Nancy, come in," Pamela said. "This is Aaron Black. Aaron, meet Nancy Colworth."

"We met the night of the break-in," Aaron said smoothly. "Can I take that for you?" he asked, motioning to the casserole.

"Yes, I brought you a tuna casserole. Even if you aren't staying here, you can take it with you," she said, handing the dish to Aaron.

"Thank you, Nancy," Pamela said, touched that her friend would take time from her busy schedule to help. "Come in and sit down—if we can sit," she said, smiling ruefully.

Nancy shook her head and ran her fingers through her black curls. "I have to pick the girls up. They're at their grandmother's and then we're going shopping for shoes, so I need to get them. Purchasing shoes for them will take us a while, and they'll wear out and get tired, so I have to run." She looked past Pamela at the apartment. "I see you're back in order."

"Such as it is," Pamela replied, watching Aaron returning from the kitchen. He looked so out of place in her tiny apartment. He belonged in a spacious house like his Pine Valley home. He wore a plaid shirt and jeans and she thought how handsome he looked and how full of vitality. It amazed her that he was still in her life and she in his. When she realized Nancy was talking, she tried to pull her attention from Aaron.

"So a few of us would like to have a party for you—sort of a house shower—when you can find time."

"Nancy, that's so sweet of you!" Pamela said, hugging her neighbor and deeply touched by the kindness of her friends. "Y'all don't have to do that."

"Of course we don't. We want to. You pick a time that's good, and we'll plan a party at my place. Give me a list of your teacher friends and anyone else you'd like to invite."

"That's so sweet," Pamela repeated, tears stinging her eyes. She was embarrassed by her emotional reaction. Aaron was beside her, his arm firmly around her waist, and she was glad for his reassuring presence.

"That's nice of you," he said in a deep voice, while she tried to pull herself together. When had she gotten so emotional over everything that happened? Was it hormones because of her pregnancy? Or the upheaval in her life caused by Aaron?

"We want to. Pamela is special. Particularly to us. The girls have little things they've made for you, but they'll want to bring them over to you. In the meantime, is there anything any of us can do to help?"

As Pamela shook her head, Aaron said, "Let me give you my phone number and pager, in case you should want to get hold of us for any reason." He pulled out a small tablet and pen and jotted down numbers, tearing out a page and handing it to Nancy.

"Call anytime you need to."

"I will. Let me know when you pick a date for a party," Nancy said.

"Thank you, and thanks for the casserole. We'll enjoy it," Pamela said, thinking about the freezer filled with casseroles at Aaron's house and his cook who came in once a week.

Closing the door behind Nancy, Pamela leaned against it and turned to face Aaron. "Friends are nice."

"You're nice," he said, placing his hands on either side of her. "Want to keep her casserole in your freezer or take it to my place?"

"We don't need it at your house, but I'd rather take it and eat it, so I can thank her and return her dish." It was difficult to think with him standing so close.

"Ready to go home?"

"Aaron, you're going to make it so hard to say goodbye," she whispered, knowing she ought to stay anywhere except his place.

"I hope I make goodbye impossible," he replied solemnly, looking at her mouth and making her ache to kiss him. What would one more kiss hurt? How many times would she ask herself that question? If they kissed, she knew he would stop, and if he didn't, she would stop before it escalated to reckless abandon. She couldn't resist winding her arms around his neck and pulling his head down to her. She stood on tiptoe and placed her mouth on his to kiss him hungrily.

His arms went around her, and he held her tightly, leaning over her to kiss her hard, passion flaring between them. Her pulse roared and she wanted him desperately, more every hour she spent with him.

In minutes she paused to whisper, "You're making it next to impossible, but someday, Aaron, I'll say goodbye and go. I promise—"

"Don't make promises you can't keep. I hope to see to it that you never go out of my life, lady," he whispered in return, turning so he leaned against the door while he kissed her. He spread his legs and pulled her up against him. She felt his hard arousal, his long lean body and legs pressed against her, while one hand slipped beneath her sweater and pushed away her bra, cupping her breast.

She moaned, wanting him, grinding her hips against him in need and feeling as if she was drowning in desire, knowing that minute by minute and kiss by kiss he was wearing away her resistance.

"We're not at my place now," he whispered, raising his head to look at her, locks of his brown hair falling over his forehead. His solemn green eyes made her heart lurch. "Marry me, Mellie," he said, and she felt as if all air had been squeezed from her lungs. She hurt, a pounding pain that hammered her. *Don't think about what might be.*

"Aaron, stop pushing. If I say yes, it'll be for the wrong reasons," she said, wanting him, certain that the wrong reasons were his, not hers. She kissed him to stop his words that tempted and held out glittering false hopes.

They stroked and kissed until he held her in his arms and her legs were locked around him, yet clothes were between them. He stopped and set her on her feet and moved away from her, crossing the room to stand with his back to her. His fists were clenched and she could hear his ragged breathing even above her own.

"We timed that right. Here comes the guy to set the alarm."

She straightened her clothing and hoped she looked composed as the doorbell rang. She swung it open to face a uniformed workman with a toolbox in his hand. She ushered him in, and, in seconds, he and Aaron were deep in discussion about the alarm.

She gave up and let Aaron take charge, amused and chagrined at how easily he stepped into her life and took over. As soon as the man was working, Aaron said he would leave for a meeting and he would come back later to pick her up.

She agreed and followed him to the door, watching him look around carefully as he stepped outside, and she realized that even when she forgot, he was always conscious that someone could be watching them.

When he returned two hours later, she showed him the new alarm, gave him the code and finally they took the casserole and left for the Royal Memorial Hospital where she went to see Lady Helena Reichard.

While Pamela talked briefly with Lady Helena, Aaron found Matt Walker and spent time with him.

The moment Pamela emerged from Lady Helena's room, Aaron and Matt appeared. She looked at the two of them, thinking Aaron looked as much a cowboy as Matt, but she knew he wasn't. And she thought that both she and Lady Helena had some very good protection, but how long could this go on? As she joined them, Aaron draped his arm across her shoulders and pulled her close against his side.

"I'm glad you're staying at Aaron's," Matt said, glancing past her toward Lady Helena's door.

"It's hard to think we might be in danger. Lady Helena is brave, and she has enough to go through without more troubles."

"She doesn't know I'm out here. I plan to see to it that she's protected," Matt said quietly, but his tone of voice sent a shiver down Pamela's spine and she knew he had that same toughness that Aaron did.

"We'll see you," Aaron said, moving away while Pamela and Matt said goodbye.

As they left the hospital, she looked up to see Aaron's gaze sweeping the area. She looked at the drive and the parking lot, people coming and going. She didn't see anything out of the ordinary, yet why did she feel as if they were being watched? Were they still being followed? Or was her imagination becoming overactive?

By the end of the week Pamela's nerves were as frazzled as shredded paper. She ached with longing to accept Aaron's declaration of love. She was unable to sleep and she had lost what little appetite she had. Drawn to him more each hour they spent together, she wanted him and loved him more than ever. At the same time, the gulf between them seemed vastly wider. During the past week Aaron had taken her to the Black ranch, the sprawling house set on windswept plains covered with cactus and mesquite. He had flown her to Dallas and Houston for dinners and dancing. His life was houses, jets and money. Her world was Royal, Texas, little children and, soon, a baby. Yet when she was with him, she forgot everything else. He was fulfilment, fun and a companion she could confide in. He was the dash missing in her life. And dancing in his arms this past week had brought back all the powerful memories of their first night together.

She wandered restlessly around the bedroom as she got dressed to go to dinner. After spending almost two weeks constantly with him, she was on fire with sheer desire. Now it was Aaron who stopped their kisses and caresses, Aaron who pulled away, and she knew he was doing it to show her that it wasn't sex that was driving him to declare his love for her.

Glancing over her shoulder at the baskets of flowers in her room, she wondered if Aaron had bought all of Handley's flower inventory. The house was filled with them and twice this week she had sent baskets to the hospital and a nursing home.

He flirted and teased. When they weren't kissing, he constantly touched her, holding her arm, playing with her hair, stroking her back until she burned with wanting him. By now everyone in Royal knew they were a couple. They were constantly out in public together, and she had given up trying to keep their relationship private.

She glanced at the closed bedroom door and thought of him in his big bed and drew a deep breath. Safe or unsafe, she needed to move home. This was torment and only made the inevitable goodbye more difficult.

And she knew there would be a goodbye. Her feelings hadn't changed about marriage. She wanted Aaron and she loved him, but she was sure about her refusal to marry. He hadn't changed her mind one iota about their future. Aaron was dating her because being together was good. They liked each other and the chemistry was volatile, but it took more than that for a family and a lasting marriage. All his declarations of love had come after he had learned about her pregnancy, not one word of love from him before.

Also, she wondered if she had simply become a challenge to him because she suspected he was accustomed to getting what he wanted out of life and ran across few obstacles.

She touched the diamond heart-shaped pendant around her neck, lifting it to look down at it. He had given it to her Valentine's night after dinner and dancing in Houston.

She shook her head and dropped the pendant against her bare skin, picking up a black dress to slip into. Today her friends had given her a party and showered her with gifts to replace what she had lost in the break-in. A few had teased her and asked when she and Aaron would be getting married, questions easy to fend off. Only her closest friend, Jessica Atkins from Midland, knew the truth about her pregnancy. Jessica was trying to help her find a teaching job for the coming year.

The new furniture was arriving next Wednesday, and then she would be able to move back into her apartment. Wednesday she would tell Aaron goodbye. She wondered if he would accept goodbye or if she would have to move to Midland. Yet would any distance stop Aaron's persistent courtship? He was a man accustomed to getting what he wanted, but sooner or later he would see that she meant what she said in her refusal to marry.

She ran her hand across her forehead, knowing she was doing the right thing. It still seemed right to her because she was sure Aaron wasn't as deeply in love as he thought. Should she give marriage to him a chance? Would love develop between them?

The questions plagued her more and more often now, but she always came back to the same answer. Aaron hadn't been in love until he discovered he would be a father. True love doesn't switch on like turning on lights.

She sighed and zipped up her dress. Another enchanting, magical evening that would tear at her emotions. Yet it would also be a precious pearl of memory that she could cling to when he was gone.

Each day she loved him more. She combed her hair, slipped into her black pumps and looked at herself in the mirror, turning to study her flat stomach that didn't reveal a trace of her pregnancy. She turned again, looking at the diamond heart sparkling against her black dress. Her reflection looked poised, happy. None of the hurt and anguish showed in her reflection.

She picked up her small black bag and left to go downstairs. She knew Aaron would be ready and waiting. As she paused at the top of the stairs, he appeared below and stopped with his hand on the newel post to look up at her, his gaze slowly drifting over her like a caress.

Conscious of his consuming gaze, she came down the steps to meet him. Her pulse raced because he was in a dark suit that emphasized his tan skin and green eyes, and he looked incredibly handsome.

"Hi, handsome," she drawled as she came within a couple of steps of him. She stopped because the steps put her on his level, and she could look directly into his eyes.

"Hi, beautiful," he answered lightly in return, but his voice was husky and passion burned in the depths of his eyes. He rested his hand on her waist and propped his foot on the second step where she stood, his thigh pressing lightly against her. "Ready to go eat?"

"Starving, actually."

"Aw, shucks. I thought of something else we could do that would be more fun," he said in a husky voice that made her instantly think of making love.

"I don't think so," she whispered, unable to get her voice. He wasn't doing anything except flirting and looking at her as if he would devour her, but she was melting inside.

"We could order dinner sent in," he suggested. He reached up to stroke her throat. "Hot kisses all over, letting go, doing what your heart wants—what mine wants. We could take all night, darlin', wild, hot loving." His hand slid down her back and over her bottom.

"Aaron, stop," she whispered in anguish.

"You're answering me without thinking. Why not, Mellie? Why not? You don't want to kiss?"

"Yes," she whispered and saw a flare of eagerness in his eyes. "No!" She put her hand lightly against his chest as he leaned toward her. "No. That isn't wise or what I want."

"Isn't what you want?"

"All right. I don't think we should whether I want to or not. Let's go to dinner," she whispered, but her heart pounded and she wanted to wrap her arms around his neck and let him carry her right back to his bed.

She received another one of his searching gazes, and she was certain he could hear her heart pounding. He ran his finger across her forehead and she realized she was damp with perspiration.

"Hot?" he asked, arching a brow.

"On fire," she answered, and his eyes darkened.

"How do you expect me to keep my distance when you give me answers like that? Lady, your heart wants the same thing mine does."

"Not heart—our bodies. This is physical."

"I won't buy that one. There's a lot more to it than physical attraction. Come on, I'll take you to dinner and tell you how much more," he said, linking his arm through hers and starting down the hall.

"Aaron, don't make this harder."

"Honey, I couldn't get any harder," he drawled and looked down at her as she walked beside him. "Want me to prove it to you?"

"No! Stop teasing me." A blush heated her cheeks.

"I can't resist. You're too solemn, and I know you're not always that way."

"We shouldn't even be together."

"Oh, yes, we should. Now and forever. You'll see."

"Do you always get your way? Is that where all your optimism comes from?"

"Nope, I don't always get my way. This time my optimism

omes from being right and knowing that sooner or later,
ou're going to see the truth.''

She shook her head. ''Where are we going tonight?''

''My brother's boat in Galveston.''

Knowing it would be another evening that would be an
nslaught against her refusal to marry, she lapsed into silence.

They flew to Houston where a limo whisked them to Gal-
eston, and they spent the evening on his brother's yacht. It
vas almost dawn when they returned to his home in Pine
Valley. She was dazzled, so in love, and she knew she would
ave been bubbling with happiness if she could just let go and
ollow her heart, but wisdom still told her that this was all
leeting and temporary.

They kissed until both were on a ragged edge and she
topped him, hurrying to her room to spend the rest of the
ight in agony, wanting him, questioning her feelings over and
ver and still coming up with the same answers. At least this
veek, she was moving home and it would end some of the
urmoil. It would also end his courtship that had been the most
xciting, joyous, thrilling time of her life. She stared into the
arkness and could see only Aaron.

Today she was moving home. Her new furniture had been
elivered yesterday and now she could once again live at her
wn place. No matter what his arguments, no matter how per-
uasive, she had to stand by her decision and begin to break
ff this constant togetherness. It was the twenty-second of
ebruary. She had been with Aaron almost a month now. For-
ver. Minutes. Could she actually make the break with him
nd survive?

Over breakfast, looking into his green eyes, it was much
ore difficult to say the words that she had rehearsed more
an a dozen times during the night.

''I'm moving home today, Aaron.''

He lowered his fork to his plate, leaving scrambled eggs
neaten. ''You're safer here, and I'd like you to stay.''

She shrugged. ''I can't stay here forever.''

"Yes, you can."

She raised her chin and inhaled. "No, I can't. I'm going home where I need to be. Even if we were going to marry— which we aren't—I would want to go home. I need to be in my own place."

He nodded. "All right. I'll take you home when you want to go. You'll still go out to dinner tonight, won't you?"

"Aaron, we're just postponing the inevitable. You're not changing my mind."

"I'm patient," he said, reaching across the table to touch her cheek. She couldn't resist, but turned to brush a kiss across his fingers. He caught her chin and turned her to look at him. "Why are you fighting what your heart wants?"

"Because I keep thinking ahead and know this isn't the marriage for you and I'm not the woman for you."

"Don't you think you should let me make that decision?"

She shook her head and stood, picking up her dishes to carry them to the sink. "No. One of us needs to think straight. I'll get my things as soon as we clean the kitchen."

"Leave the kitchen. I'll have someone here to clean this afternoon."

She turned to look at him. "Just like that?"

"Just like that."

She put down the dishes and left the room, and Aaron watched her go, wondering how long it would take to get her to listen to her heart and really listen to what he was saying to her. He knew she had been hurt badly when she was growing up, and old hurts were slow to mend, but he thought he was making progress. He looked at his knuckles and remembered her soft lips pressed against them when she had turned to kiss him. "Patience, man," he whispered. "Patience."

After dinner that night Aaron took her key to unlock the door to her apartment. He hadn't spotted a tail all evening, nor could he see anyone lurking in the shadows. "I'm going to look around," he said, stepping inside and turning off the new alarm. "You wait here."

Pamela hung up her coat and watched him prowl through the apartment. Tonight they'd driven to a honky-tonk outside Royal for some two-stepping music and barbecue. She wore jeans and a red sweater. He was in his black boots, a black wool shirt and jeans, and just the sight of him made her pulse race. She was going to miss him and knew in a few minutes he would kiss her good-night and be gone.

He came back and headed for the front door. "I'm going to look around outside. I have your key, so lock up behind me and turn on the alarm."

"I'm not real happy to think about you prowling around out there in the dark."

He crossed to her and brushed a kiss on her lips. "Uncle Sam taught me how to get around in the dark and take care of myself. And I grew up out here with the rattlesnakes, so I'll be careful."

She couldn't laugh at his casual remarks that were meant to reassure her. She watched him leave and followed him, locking the door and resetting the alarm. She paced the floor until she heard the key in the lock and he stepped inside. It had been thirty minutes since he left.

"All quiet on the home front," he said, tossing the key on a table, turning off the alarm and crossing the room to sweep her up into his arms.

"Aaron!" she cried, hugging his neck as he swung her around.

"You look far too solemn. I liked it better when we were two-stepping tonight and you were laughing and your dimples were showing." He carried her to the sofa and in minutes they were locked in an embrace. She had stopped thinking about all the reasons she shouldn't kiss him, instead giving herself up to the kisses they shared, because usually he stopped sooner than she would have. This time when he did, he stroked her hair from her face while their erratic hearts slowed, and they caught their breath.

"Well, I wish you'd stay at my house, but if not—here we are."

Startled, she stopped straightening her sweater and looked at him in surprise. "No."

"We're not going to argue this one, lady. You're staying here. I'm staying here. Until I think you're completely out of danger, I'm your shadow."

"Aaron, I don't have another bedroom."

"You have a couch. We're sitting on it."

"Look at it. It's not long enough for you!"

"Well, now there's another possibility," he drawled, his green eyes smoldering.

"No way!" she snapped, knowing he was teasing, yet aware he was watching her closely. "All right, just stay on the couch and get kinks in your neck and back. This is crazy, Aaron."

"Need I remind you that your apartment has been broken into?"

Her emotions churned as she had a vivid memory of her trashed apartment. Yet how could Aaron stay here in her tiny apartment? "Okay, stay. I'll get you a blanket and pillows." She left, dismayed to find she was going to have him living with her. She knew the only way she would get him out of her apartment was to go home with him. At her place, more people were going to see them together and realize he was staying there. In some ways, she preferred the privacy of his place. Reluctantly, she gathered up bedding and took it back to him.

He had shed his shirt and boots and belt, the jeans riding low on his narrow hips. Her mouth went dry at the sight of his bare chest, and she paused, assaulted by memories of how his naked body had felt against hers, how he had felt inside her.

"For me?" he asked as if nothing had changed, yet his voice had dropped a notch and he was watching her with that hawklike intensity as he crossed the room to take the pillow and blankets from her. He tossed them onto the sofa and turned to pull her into his arms. "I'll win you over," he whispered before he leaned down to kiss her, "because half of you

s already on my side. Your heart wants the same thing I do.
Sooner or later your head is going to listen to your heart and
o what I'm telling you and hear the truth.''

"Aaron—"

His kiss shut off the world and she was lost, melting into
his arms and welcoming his embrace. She slid her hands over
his warm, bare back that was smooth as silk. She hated the
ayers of clothing still between them. Then his hands slipped
beneath her sweater. Swiftly he unfastened her bra and pushed
away the lace, cupping her breast while his thumb moved in
azy circles over her nipple.

Sensations assaulted her, and desire became molten heat in
her veins. Moaning softly, she arched against him, wanting
him, her hands caressing his smooth back.

When he stepped away, desire was blatant in his hungry
gaze. "To prove a point to you, I'll wait to make love to you.
I love you, Mellie, now and always."

"Aaron," she said, hurting, wanting him, knowing he was
as tormented as she, yet still certain she was right. "You
shouldn't stay here, and we should stop kisses that can only
lead to heartache."

"I'm staying, lady. There's only one way to get me out of
here."

"Aaron, this is insane. We'll bump into each other constantly. I only have one bathroom."

"Want to go to my place?"

"No!" she cried in exasperation. "You'll get tired of this
fast," she muttered darkly.

"Never as long as you're here," he answered with such
cheer that she gritted her teeth.

Within ten minutes she had decided she might have been
better off going back to his place. Her apartment was tiny and
didn't give them the privacy his spacious mansion had. She
yanked on her fuzzy robe, remembering his elegant navy velvet robe and headed for the bathroom only to stop when she
heard the shower running and Aaron singing lustily.

Visions of him taunted her because they had showered together that first night. She ground her teeth together and rushed to the kitchen, getting down cups and fixing hot chocolate and trying to stop thinking about Aaron naked in her shower.

"Can I help?" he asked.

He wore jeans again that rode low on his hips. His chest and feet were bare and her mouth went dry. She couldn't stop her gaze from drifting down over his muscled chest tapering to a slim waist. Her gaze flew back up to meet a mocking look in his eyes as he crossed the room with deliberation. Narrowing the distance between them to inches, he took a cup of chocolate from her hands and set it on the sink without taking his eyes from hers. Her pulse drummed as he moved close. She was pressed against the kitchen counter, looking up at him. His green eyes held such blatant desire that her knees weakened. He ran his fingers through her hair and framed her face with his hands and she knew from looking into his eyes what he was going to say before he ever uttered a word.

Eight

"I've waited, Mellie. I've waited damned long so you'd have
to know it isn't just sex driving me." His voice was hoarse
and low, almost a whisper and his eyes sent a message that
scalded her. "I want you and I love you. There's love in my
heart or I wouldn't have waited. Love and respect, Mellie, love
is enduring as the Texas sunshine."

"Aaron..." she whispered. She should say no. He placed
her hand against his chest, and she could feel his racing heart,
and she knew her own was racing equally fast.

"Feel my heart—you excite me in a way no woman ever
has. I want you forever, my partner, my friend, my wife. I
know this is right and good. And I know, deep in your heart,
it's what we both want."

"It can't be," she whispered, his words becoming etched
in her memory and her heart. She was lost, knowing she
couldn't resist him this night, and that she didn't want to.

Tossing aside all wisdom and caution and reserve, she let
go. "For now, Aaron, I can't tell you no." She slipped her

arms around his neck and turned loose all her pent-up frustrations and longing.

Before his head lowered and his mouth covered hers, she saw the flare of eagerness in his eyes. Their tongues met and stroked and she gave in to all the impulses and desires she had fought for so long. Her hands slipped over him, rediscovering his marvelous body, lean, muscled and hard. She tangled her fingers in the mat of hair on his chest, then let her hand drift down over his flat belly.

He made a rough noise deep in his throat and crushed her in his arms, leaning over her and kissing her deeply. Their tongues stroked and then his plunged in an age-old rhythm, stopping and teasing, flicking against the tip of her tongue. She moaned with pleasure while her roaring pulse shut out all other sounds.

She pushed back to look at him. "This doesn't change anything."

"Yeah, sure," he drawled in a husky voice as he pushed her robe off her shoulders and peeled away the cotton nightie. She knew her words were only a half truth. His loving couldn't change what she thought she ought to do, but it would change the depth of her love for him. More than ever, her love for him would deepen.

"You're beautiful," he whispered while his hands cupped her breasts and he bent his head to stroke her nipple with his tongue. As he kissed and teased, his thumb drew slow circles on her other nipple and delicious sensations tormented and rocked her.

When she unbuttoned his jeans and shoved them away, her fingers shook with urgency. She pushed away his briefs and freed him, taking him in her hand.

Aaron's pulse roared, and his heart pounded violently. He knew that for tonight, she had thrown aside her refusal to love. *Now, now…* The words played in the back of his mind. *Now I can show you how I love you.* He wanted to say the words to her, but his voice failed him, and only a low growl in his throat came as her hand stroked him.

He knew she had no idea how she affected him. That she could turn him to jelly, scramble his thoughts all during the day when she was completely across town from him. He knew she didn't think of herself as beautiful, but to him, she was the most beautiful woman he had ever known. He loved her slender, soft body with its curves and feminine secrets. He loved her wanton passion, her eager responses to his slightest caress. He loved her laughter, her caring.

He was going to have to stop her caresses because he wanted to last far into the night, to make love to her until she was wild with need—until she felt the way he did. He wanted to devour her, to kiss every inch of her, stroke and love her and try to show her in a million different ways how he loved her.

And he wanted to bind her heart to his irrevocably, drowning all her foolishness and convincing her that his heart was in his words and that he had thought everything through. Damned if he didn't know his own feelings!

She was the woman for him. He didn't have a shred of doubt, and every kiss made him want her more than ever. She was a marvel to him, a mystery, as necessary as breathing for him to survive. He couldn't think about life without her. He wouldn't accept defeat in this affair that was the most important thing in his life.

In government, he had had irrevocable rejections, stalemates, severing of ties, and he knew how to pick up the broken pieces and go on with life. But not here, not when the pieces were his heart and when his life and future were at stake. Here he couldn't accept defeat. Especially not when he thought his lady really wanted the same thing he did, but was afraid to let go and trust. Old hurts tormented her and jaded her views, but he would see the truth.

Too much was at stake for him to give in to her steady refusals: their future, their baby, their lives together. This passion that was beyond his widest imaginings.

With a groan he picked her up, sweeping her into his arms to carry her to her bed. The only light was a small lamp on a bedside table that shed a warm glow over their naked bodies. He lowered her to the bed, shoving the mound of lacy white pillows to the floor as he moved to her feet. With deliberation, watching her, he trailed kisses along her slender foot and ankle while his other hand stroked her smooth leg.

Tingles radiated from each kiss and caress, and Pamela gazed into his eyes while he kissed her.

"I love you," he said hoarsely. "Every inch of you."

"Aaron," she gasped, reaching for him and tangling her fingers in his hair. She started to sit up, to try to pull him to her, but he gently pushed her down.

"Let me kiss you, Mellie. I want to kiss you all night long. I want you to want to make love as much as I want to make love."

Her heart thudded at the look in his eyes and the words he whispered to her. His green eyes held a hunger that made her feel every word he spoke was the truth. Trailing kisses along her inner leg, he moved higher to the sensitive inside of her thigh.

"Aaron," she said, her eyes closing while passion rocked her. She grasped his shoulders, tugging to pull him to her, but he continued brushing kisses along her thigh while his hand lightly caressed her, touching the sensitive center of her femininity between her legs, driving her crazy with need. He watched her steadily, while he kissed her inner thigh, the stubble of his beard faintly tickling her.

"Aaron," she cried his name again, trying to sit up to reach him, but he pushed gently.

"Let me kiss you the way I want to," he urged, and then his head dipped between her thighs, his tongue following where his hand had been, his tongue stroking, driving her to an even higher threshold of need. She moaned, losing awareness of anything except his touch while she moved against him and all she knew was his hands and his tongue.

As her hands slid over his broad shoulders, she spread her legs, opening herself to him completely, yielding and clinging to his shoulders. She wound her fingers through his short, thick hair and she arched her back. His loving drove her closer and closer to a brink.

"Aaron, please," she gasped, moving against him, on fire with need, taut and trembling.

"We've just started," he whispered. "Before this night is over, you'll want to love as badly as I want to."

"I do want to. I want you!" she cried, in a frenzy already, wanting him desperately, driven to such urgency she thought she would fly apart any minute. "Aaron!" she gasped, coming up to shove him down and move astride him, pressing her knees against his hips. She leaned down, taking his manhood in her mouth, to kiss and drive him to the same brink of desire. He lay beneath her, watching her, his hand tangled in her hair and his other hand stroking her hip. She looked at his tanned body against the snow-white comforter covering her bed, his masculinity so blatant, so marvelous.

He was so out of place in her bed and in her life. Yet how wonderful to have him here, beneath her, his hands touching her. He was bare for her, letting her kiss and touch him, explore and memorize, letting her love him as she had dreamed of each night since their first time together.

For only seconds more he let her caress him, and then she was in his arms, looking up at him as he leaned down to kiss her more hungrily than before. She wound her arm around his neck, running her fingers through his hair, her other hand resting on his waist.

Aaron cradled her against him, caressing her with his free hand, cupping the soft fulness of her breast. His mouth muffled her moan. Sweat dotted his forehead and he shook with the effort to maintain his control because he wanted to keep loving her far into the night.

"Aaron, love me," she whispered, wanting him completely.

"We've just started loving," he whispered, showering her with kisses along her ear and throat and then moving her, rolling her onto her stomach. "Let me kiss you all night," he whispered, trailing kisses on the back of her leg, up behind her knee while his hands stroked her. She moaned and spread her legs for him as he kissed her thighs and his hand slid over her bottom.

She flung herself over and pulled him down. "Come here, Aaron. You're driving me wild," she whispered fiercely, pulling his head down to kiss him as if it were the last kiss of her life.

It was almost an hour before she leaned over him, caressing him, her hand closing on his thick, hot manhood. She moved closer to trail her tongue over the velvet tip, to take him in her mouth as his hand caressed her legs and then touched the magic center of her, rubbing and driving her into oblivion again, pushing her to another brink as he had countless times during the night. She moved against him, kissing him and yielding to abandon.

"Don't stop," she whispered. "I want you. I want you…" Her voice trailed away and she gasped, her body tightening as an explosion of release came, her hips moving convulsively, and then she wanted him more than ever, desperately needing him.

She shifted, moving over him. "Now, Aaron. I won't wait."

His eyes were dark as obsidian. Glittering green turned black by hot desire. He rolled them over so she was beneath him as he moved between her legs.

She looked at him poised over her and knew she would never forget this moment. He was hard, his shaft thick and dark, springing from a mass of thick hair. Short hairs covered his strong thighs and his body glowed with vitality. Love surged in her along with a consuming physical need. "Come here, Aaron," she said, pulling on his hips, running her hands over his tight bottom, hard and smooth. She wrapped her long legs around him and tried to pull him down.

His gaze ran over her slowly. "You're so beautiful," he said roughly, lowering himself.

As the tip of his shaft pressed against her, she reached to hold him, to guide him, but he caught her hands and teased her while her hips thrashed and arched. "Aaron!"

"You want all this, don't you?" he whispered. "And it's good, isn't it?"

"Yes! Oh, yes."

Then he slipped into her, filling her slowly, hot and hard. She cried out in eagerness, her hips rising to meet him as he came down over her and kissed her, stopping her cries.

They moved together, united at last, and she relished it, giving completely, wild with wanting him. Her world narrowed to his marvelous body that drove her to a frenzy. And beneath all the passion was the knowledge that she was once again in his arms, loving him and being loved by him, united with him with no restrictions.

Eternity was now, this moment only. Thought swirled away, lost in the most urgent, primal dance. "Mellie!" Aaron cried, his voice guttural and hoarse. "My love."

"Ah, Aaron," she whispered. "How I love you!"

He kissed her as they moved together until she crashed over a brink, climaxing with a cry of ecstasy while he thrust hard and fast and she could feel the hot burst of his climax within her. And then she was carried away on another wild, swift climb into another burst of rapturous release.

Her return to reality was gradual while their pounding hearts slowed. She was aware of Aaron showering her with light kisses, holding her close in his arms. He rolled onto his side, taking her with him, while he stroked her hair away from her face. Their bodies were damp, sated with love. How perfect it seemed to be with him.

"I love you," he whispered.

"Aaron—"

"Shh." He placed his fingers on her lips. "Let's let tonight be something special like that first night was."

She tightened her arms around him and placed her head against his chest, willing to do what he wanted for now. She agreed with him to drop worries about the future. Tomorrow would come soon enough. At the moment she would take tonight like that first night as something very special and unique and unforgettable. His heartbeat was steady and strong. His arms held her close, and their legs were entwined. She was wrapped in bliss.

"You're magic in my life," he whispered. Relishing the words, she knew she would remember them always. "I've wanted this every night since that first night."

"You couldn't have!" she said, surprised and questioning.

"I did. Why do you think I came back from Spain? Why do you think you were important to me when the only time we had been together was that one night?"

She wanted to believe him, yet she couldn't. Their first night was a night of passion that they both got caught up in, and she still couldn't believe that it had been important to him. He hadn't tried to call or get in touch with her except right after the plane's forced landing.

She kissed him, wanting to keep touching him, to stay in his arms forever, wishing the moment they would have to separate would never come.

"I wish I had you all to myself, and we could stay here all day tomorrow without any interruptions. We could fly to Dallas—"

"Stop planning. No, we can't. You said we'd take tonight as something special. Tomorrow you and I both have things we have to do."

"Maybe. But I know what I'd prefer." He shifted away and stood, scooping her into his arms. "Let's try out that shower of yours again."

"Oh, Aaron!" she exclaimed, remembering the last shower with him and the lovemaking they had shared. He carried her the short distance to her tiny bathroom and in minutes they were in her shower over the bathtub, Aaron slowly soaping her up, sliding his hands over her wet skin. She took the soap from him to do the same, running her hands over his broad, muscled back, down to his smooth backside and then along his thighs. He turned to face her and as she moved up, she saw he was ready to love again, fully aroused. She looked up at him and met a smoldering gaze that heated her to her core.

He took the soap from her hands and let the spray wash

over them as he lifted her up. She locked her long legs around him and he eased her down, sliding into her and then she was spun away, the dance of ecstasy starting as she clung to him and kissed him.

While he braced his feet apart and held her, he pumped and ground his hips and knew he couldn't get enough of her in a lifetime. With the slightest touch or look from her, he was aroused. Being with her naked and knowing she would yield had him tied in knots. He knew he should be sated, worn and satisfied from their last session of lovemaking, but he wasn't. He wanted her more than ever. She couldn't get it through her head how much and how deeply he loved her, but she would. She had to. If it took him the rest of the year, he wasn't giving up because he wanted her with his whole being.

She was kissing him, hot kisses that felt as if they would melt his teeth and his tonsils. She was fiery, passionate, totally giving when aroused and that excited him even more.

Thought ceased and he loved her blindly, mindlessly, this time hard and fast and reaching a roaring climax. Dimly he heard her cries of passion, felt her fingers dig into his back and her legs tighten around him.

His heart pounded as if it would explode in his chest and even under a stream of water, he was sweating.

Gradually she slid down, standing on her feet while they kissed. He couldn't stop kissing her or holding her. She was slender and soft in his arms, her skin smoother than satin. He framed her face with his hands. "You're beautiful."

"You're blind, Aaron, but I'm glad you think so. I'm glad you're holding me. Otherwise I think I'd just slide down and go into the drain with the water."

"Let's see if I've still got legs I can walk on." He shut off the water and opened the shower door, grabbing a towel to dry her. She took the towel from him.

"Maybe I should do this, and you should dry yourself off."

He looked at her, seeing fires still burning in her blue eyes. "You really think so?"

She studied him, her gaze drifting down over him and back

up and she shook her head, beginning to dry him with the towel. She slanted him a mischievous look.

"Let's see what happens."

"Insatiable minx," he whispered, bending down to kiss her. He grabbed another towel and slowly drew it across her shoulders, then leaned back to look at her as he ran it so lightly across her breasts, just touching her nipples and seeing them become taut. He drew the towel down across her stomach and then over her bottom.

"Aaron," she whispered, winding her arms around his neck and pulling his head down to kiss him. They attempted to dry each other until he picked her up to carry her back to her bed where he lay down and pulled her into his arms, and they kissed slowly, leisurely, stroking each other. Within minutes fires built and urgency drove them.

Finally she sat astride him, lowering herself while he caressed her breasts, and then she leaned down to kiss him, moving with him. After they had reached another rapturous climax, he pulled her beside him, cradling her in his arms, talking softly until they fell asleep.

In the gray light of dawn Aaron came awake, staring at the pink rosebuds in her wallpaper, remembering clearly where he was and what had happened between them. He looked down at her, still asleep in the crook of his arm.

"This time you won't disappear, darlin'," he said softly. She lay with one arm thrown across his chest and her leg across him. He gently brushed her hair away from her face, and, with just the sight of her and his memories, he was aroused, wanting her as badly as he had yesterday.

He stroked her breast so lightly, caressing her soft nipple until it became taut. She moaned and stirred and opened her eyes to look up at him. He saw she was completely awake, a lazy sensuality radiating from her like heat from a stove. She wrapped one arm around his neck and raised to kiss him while her hand played over his stomach, caressing his thighs and then touching his manhood.

In minutes they were loving with all the urgency of the

night before. Aaron knew the day would intrude and end their intimacy, and he slowed, trying to prolong the moment, wanting to savor every inch of her and every moment with her.

Finally he moved between her legs, wrapping her in his arms as he entered her and her legs locked around him. While they loved passionately, he heard her crying his name. He climaxed and slowly settled, showering her with kisses, amazed how the more he made love with her, the more he wanted her.

"You're easy to wake."

She trailed kisses along his throat. "That's the best way to wake, Aaron."

"Maybe. Maybe there's some way even better. I'll show you in the morning."

"No, you won't either," she said, her fingers playing in the hair on his chest.

"Mellie, I'm going to shrivel up and blow away. You've demolished me."

"Are you complaining about what I'm doing?" she asked, raising up to look at him with wide blue eyes. A dimple showed, and she lowered her head. "Just lie back and enjoy the morning. Go back to sleep," she whispered, trailing kisses along his stomach, laughing seductively when he became aroused again.

"Wench," he growled, rolling her over on her back and moving over her with his legs on either side of her. "Two can play that game." He leaned down to kiss her, his hand moving between her legs. She gasped and opened her legs for him and in minutes they were loving again.

Wrapped in each other's arms, they fell asleep. Aaron came awake instantly at the ring of his cell phone. It was a faint sound and he slid out of bed and hurried to the front room where he had left the phone on a table. He picked it up.

"Aaron? Sheriff Escobar. You wanted me to call you when we got a report in on the Asterland plane. The feds finished their investigation."

Nine

Two hours later on Thursday morning, Aaron sat in the Texas Cattleman's Club in the private room he and his friends used. Coffee had been served and a silver urn sat on a table on a silver tray. Bone china cups and saucers with the club's gold crest sat beside the urn.

Matt Walker was the last to arrive, and, as he sat down facing them, Aaron leaned forward. "Before we get down to business—I think we should congratulate the new bridegroom," he said, looking at Justin, who grinned and accepted congratulations and a few teasing remarks.

"Winona and I just wanted a quiet wedding," he said. "We didn't want to be away from Angel," he added, fishing a picture from his wallet. When the others crowded around to look at the picture of the tiny blue-eyed baby girl, Aaron's insides knotted. He ached for his own baby, thinking that falling in love and having a baby with Pamela were the most awesome events in his life. *He couldn't lose her and his baby.* He refused to accept that she would do what she threatened and walk out of his life. It was unthinkable.

"She's beautiful," he said hoarsely, touching the corner of Angel's picture. He looked up. "You're a lucky man," he said solemnly, and Justin grinned.

"I know I am."

Aaron turned away, but he saw Matt give him a searching look.

"You went from a bachelor to a husband and father in a hurry," Ben Rassad said.

"Yes, and it's great."

Aaron thought of Pamela and their baby and could understand the sparkle in Justin's eyes. He looked happier than Aaron could recall ever seeing him, and Aaron was glad for him.

After getting refills of coffee and hearing a little about Angel, they sat down again, except for Dakota who stood beside a bookcase. "What's up, Aaron?" he asked.

"I had a call from Sheriff Escobar. The investigation about the cause of the crash is over. It was a malfunction in one of the twin jet engines."

"No sabotage?" Justin asked with disbelief in his voice.

"Nope." Aaron shook his head. "The engine fire caused some of the systems to lock up, including the landing gear, which caused the crash landing. When they landed, the electrical systems inside the plane shorted out. Liquor bottles from the bar broke and spilled—"

"And Lady Helena was unfortunate enough to be sitting closest to the bar," Matt interrupted grimly.

"Right," Aaron replied. "They think sparks from the rough landing ignited the liquor, and that's how she got burned."

"Damn," Matt muttered, rubbing the knee of his jeans idly as he stared into space with troubled eyes, and Aaron knew he was concerned about Lady Helena.

"At least now we have one bit of the puzzle solved," Dakota said, moving restlessly at one end of the room.

"If the plane hadn't had trouble, we wouldn't have found the stones," Justin added.

"We can stop worrying about who might have sabotaged the plane and why," Aaron summed up. "It's one little question answered. The other questions are still puzzling, and I think the women are still in danger. With the murder of Riley Monroe, we know someone is in deadly earnest about the jewels."

"A man tried to get into Lady Helena's room," Matt said. "I had to leave for just a few minutes, and the guy I got to stand watch was called away. He was only gone minutes. While he was gone, I came back, and another man was starting into her room. He ran when he saw me."

"Damn. Sounds like the one trailing after Pamela. Did you get a good look at him?" Aaron asked, and Matt shook his head.

"No. It was late and the lights were down in the hall so the patients could sleep. He was gone in a flash, and it was more important to check on her and stay with her than to go after him. She was asleep and didn't know anything happened. She didn't know I checked to see if she was all right. I couldn't leave her unguarded to chase him."

"Yeah," Aaron replied, thinking about seeing someone following Pamela outside the obstetrician's office and making the same decision to stay with her.

"If someone is getting more desperate about the missing diamond," Ben observed, "the risk for these women may be increasing."

"And we don't have any leads on the missing diamond," Dakota said quietly.

"You were going to keep an eye on the Asterland investigators. What about them, Dakota?" Aaron asked.

Dakota shook his head. "They've split up, so I have to choose which one I follow. So far nothing has come of it. One was behind you when you and Pamela were going to dinner, but I don't know whether he was actually following you or just driving down Main. Before you turned into Claire's lot, he drove into the gas station."

"If you can, keep watching them," Justin urged. "We need to find out who's after the women."

"We need to find out a lot of things," Aaron said.

"Robert Klimt is still in a coma. If he ever comes out of the coma, I hope we can question him," Matt said. "And there's always the possibility that one of the women might have the diamond and not know it."

"I don't think it's Pamela. They shredded everything she owned and didn't find what they were searching for," Aaron stated, remembering her apartment and clothing.

"Think that might have been Johannes and Yungst?" Dakota asked.

"Could be. Although anyone would want the jewels," Aaron said.

"I still wonder if whoever is after them intends to sell them and use the money for something else," Dakota remarked curtly.

"That's what I'm thinking," Aaron agreed.

"Perhaps in your diplomatic job you have dealt with espionage and terrorism too much," Ben said. "We know Dakota has."

"My mind may run that way because of all I've seen. The possibility exists that it's more than just the fortune from the jewels that someone is after. They may have a use for the fortune and it may be tied to Asterland. I wonder if we shouldn't call in a foreign affairs specialist," Aaron suggested quietly. Dakota's head whipped around, and he stared at Aaron who gazed back steadily.

Aaron had been overseas when Dakota's breakup came from his wife, Kathy Lewis, and he knew they both still hurt over it. A former Foreign Service Officer, Kathy was an expert foreign affairs specialist and Aaron knew she was well acquainted with Asterland royalty. She might be able to help them with their questions. Yet he could see the pain in Dakota's eyes over his suggestion.

"No need to rush into that yet," Justin said, and Aaron nodded. He didn't want to hurt Dakota, yet he didn't think Dakota had ever lost his love for Kathy, and he hadn't heard of Kathy being involved with anyone else since she'd left Dakota. He hoped they could get back together because both seemed to still be hurting, and he understood that kind of pain. He thought of Pamela and glanced at his watch, calculating the time until he would be with her again.

Dakota said, "We'll all keep searching and looking and seeing what we can learn."

"I want to talk to the Asterland investigators," Aaron said. "I think it's time we asked them some direct questions."

"If that's it, I need to get back to the hospital," Matt said, standing. The others came to their feet, murmuring reasons they had to go.

Aaron met Matt's gaze and could see the worry in his eyes. He could understand Matt's feelings because he was concerned about Pamela any time he was away from her. He had been much less worried when she had been at his house where there was a guard at the gate, a high wall, an alarm and seclusion. Her apartment complex had almost as many people coming and going as a shopping mall, and there was no security, but he knew he wasn't going to get her back to his place easily.

In spite of feeling a sense of urgency to get back to Pamela, he stopped at a jewelry store to look at diamond rings. He wanted something special for Pamela, knowing she seldom wore jewelry, and that what she wore was simple. He settled on a design of smaller diamonds flanking a three-carat diamond and on impulse bought her as well a simple gold link bracelet.

He drove home to take care of some family business and to make an appointment to talk to the Asterland investigators. When he stepped into his empty house, he suffered a pang. It was the first time he'd come home since Pamela had moved out and he missed her. He looked at flowers she had left behind because there wasn't room for all the bouquets at her place. He missed her with a hungry longing that made him

ant to toss aside all he needed to do and go find her. He
icked up the phone to call her, and the moment he heard her
oice, he felt better.

"I miss you."

She laughed softly. "It's only been a few hours, but that's
ce and I miss you, too."

"Can I pick you up for lunch? Say yes."

"Yes, but I have to get a haircut at three o'clock. I need to
n some errands, too, so either I meet you for lunch or you
ing me home afterwards to get my car."

"I'll take you home after lunch. I'll be at your house at—"
paused to glance at his watch "—at twelve."

"Sure, Aaron. I'll be ready."

"I'll be ready, too," he said in a husky voice, wanting to
ke her to bed again.

"Ready for lunch," she said emphatically.

"We'll see, darlin'," he challenged. "'Til then I'll think
out last night."

"And this morning," she added softly. "Hurry home,
aron," she said in a sultry voice, and heat flashed in his
dy.

"I'll be there in twenty minutes," he said, deciding to make
me of his phone calls later.

"See you," she said softly and broke the connection.

He replaced the receiver. "I wish you could see what's in
ur heart, darlin'," he said to the empty room. He thought
out the night and her complete abandon, her loving him as
her love for him was total. "You have to see what you
ean to me," he said softly. "You have to." He thought
out Justin's glow and could understand how Justin felt. To
married to the woman you love and adore and to have a
ecious baby would be the kind of happiness to make a man
ow. And it would be a glow that would go deep, clear to
heart. "You just have to see I mean what I say, lady," he
eated to the empty room, thinking of Pamela.

"Patience, patience," he reminded himself as he went up-
irs to his desk to make his calls.

* * *

Pamela had a long lunch with Aaron in which he flirted constantly and kept touching her instead of eating. He left his lunch almost untouched, just as she did, and she was giddy from his attention. She drifted through the afternoon in a daze, and as she stepped out of the shop after getting her hair cut she saw Winona Raye only a few feet away on the sidewalk. In Winona's arms was a baby carrier, and Pamela's heart beat faster.

"Congratulations on your marriage, Winona."

"Thanks," Winona said, and Pamela saw the sparkle in her eyes and had a pang of longing that stabbed into her heart like a knife for what could never be.

She moved closer to Winona to peer into the carrier. "May I see Angel?"

As she turned so Pamela could look into the carrier, Winona smiled. "How are you doing? Did you get over your injuries from the landing?"

"Yes. I wasn't seriously hurt." Pamela looked at the baby who gazed back with wide blue eyes. "She's so beautiful!"

"I think so," Winona said softly with a laugh. "Angel is a joy."

"I know she's in her carrier, but can I hold her?" Pamela said, unable to keep the longing out of her voice.

"Of course," Winona said, setting the carrier down and bending down to unfasten the straps. She handed Angel to Pamela, who took the warm, soft baby and held her close.

"She's wonderful," Pamela said, her imagination racing away with her as she thought of her own baby. *Hers and Aaron's.* "I know you're so happy."

Winona laughed. "Here, let me give you a blanket to put on your shoulder. Just in case—"

"She's fine," Pamela said, turning the baby to cradle her in her arms and look down at her. Angel cooed and waved her fists, and Pamela knew she was keeping them out in the wind and she needed to hand Angel back. Reluctantly, she passed the baby back to Winona.

"Thanks for letting me hold her," she said as Winona
uickly fastened Angel back into her carrier and picked it up.

"Anytime. Come see us and you can hold her all you
ant."

Pamela wanted to offer to babysit, but she knew right now
as not the time to do so.

"See you," Winona said, moving on and Pamela turned
vay, thinking about Angel and how precious a baby was.
he'd walked a few yards, starting to go to the driver's side
f her car, when she saw a man leaning against the door of
er car. As she approached him, he straightened up. A version
led her when she recognized Garth Johannes. A fedora was
mmed on his head, the spiky ends of his greasy hair sticking
it beneath his hat, and in a topcoat he looked square. His
ick neck bulged over the collar of his shirt.

"Miss Miles. I haven't seen you in town very often in the
ist few weeks. Shut away with your lover?"

The question was personal, and the man was obnoxious, and
e suspected if Aaron were present, Johannes would never
ive been so bold. His gaze raked insolently over her. He
ocked her from getting into her car, but she didn't feel any
ar, standing on Main Street in Royal. Anger was her only
action.

"You're in my way."

"I just wanted to ask you a few more questions."

"I've answered all I intend to," she replied curtly. Out of
e corner of her eye she saw a red pickup sweep into a park
g space a few cars beyond hers. Johannes turned to look at

"Then I'll ask you another time," he said abruptly, and
ned to hurry across the street, almost stepping in front of
ffic in his haste to move away from her car. She glanced
ck at the pickup as a door slammed and a tall, black-haired
in emerged. She didn't know Dakota Lewis very well, but
y had met, and she recognized him. She guessed he had
pped because of Johannes.

"Hi, Pamela," he said easily, but his eyes held a coldness

that she wouldn't want to be on the wrong side of as his gaze followed Johannes hurrying across the street. "Did he bother you? I can go after him."

"No, Dakota. Thanks for stopping. He's gone now. He wanted to ask me some more questions, but I told him I wasn' answering any more."

"Good. Aaron's at the Wrangler Drilling Company in a meeting. I can page him—"

"Good heavens, no! Aaron would tear up the town to go after the man, and it's not necessary. I'm glad you stopped though. Thanks. I'll go on home, and there's no need to let Aaron know. I'll tell him tonight when I see him."

Suddenly Dakota's gaze flickered back to her briefly, and amusement flashed in his dark eyes. "No deal. I'll tell Aaron before tonight, or he'll have my neck for not letting him know that that guy was bothering you. I think I'll see where the creep is going. Sure you're all right?"

"I'm fine. See you later, Dakota."

He was already gone, striding across the street. She went to her car and slid inside, shivering. Johannes was creepy, and she really would rather Aaron didn't know about the incident at all, but Dakota was going to tell him.

She was getting ready for her dinner date with Aaron that evening, dressing in jeans and a red sweater, when she heard the key turn in the lock, and then he stepped inside. "Hi honey, I'm home," he called, and she smiled as she left the bedroom to meet him. He wore jeans, a white shirt and his black Stetson and her heart jumped at the sight of him.

"The cowboy diplomat," she said, crossing the room to him and walking into his arms, her pulse jumping another notch at the hungry look in his eyes.

"You look beautiful," he whispered, before he leaned down to kiss her. When his mouth touched hers, desire ballooned within her. Tightening her arms around his neck, she stopped thinking about the future, once again clinging to the moment, loving him with her whole heart and soul.

"Ahh, darlin'," he whispered as he trailed kisses along her throat and his hands slipped beneath her sweater, unfastening the clasp to her lacy bra and cupping her breasts. She moaned softly, her hands tugging at the buttons on his shirt, and all she wanted was to be in his arms, loving him and letting him love her.

They left a trail of clothes to her bedroom, where Aaron picked her up to carry her the rest of the way to her bed, and then she was in his arms as if it were the first time all over again. Need drove her and she pushed him down on the bed, trailing kisses over his chest and down his flat stomach, down to his manhood. He caught her beneath the arms and rolled her over, moving on top of her and the sight of him poised above her made her tremble with hot desire for all of him.

"I want you so badly, Aaron," she whispered.

He lowered himself, slowly easing into her. "Never can you want me the way I want you, love. Never." His green eyes were dark as night with hot pinpoints of fiery longing. He moved slowly within her and she moved with him, her hips raising as her legs tightened around him.

While her pulse roared and sensations rocked her, she closed her eyes. All the time, she reveled that Aaron was in her arms, Aaron was loving her and she was his love once again.

They climaxed and drifted back slowly to reality. He held her close against him, stroking her and showering her with light kisses.

"I love you, Mellie," he said. "Love you with all my heart."

She closed her eyes and buried her face against his chest and hurt. Why hadn't she been careful that first time? They might have had a chance, but this way, she still couldn't believe that what he felt was anything but infatuation, passion, a relationship ruled by great sex and some fun times together. But there was more to life than that. And they weren't living in a real world, staying together at his place or at her place, neither of them working or dealing with everyday life. How could she fit into his life?

She couldn't. The answer was always the same. She couldn't see herself married to a diplomat. She had no background for his life.

He shifted and tilted her chin up, his green eyes stormy. "What're you thinking, darlin'?"

"I'm thinking some day you'll wake up and see our relationship the way I see it. I don't fit into your lifestyle, Aaron."

"You belong in my life because I want you there, not because of some set of rules."

She knew they were going to get nowhere with this argument and she turned away. "You said something about dinner."

"Sure did," he said cheerfully and scooped her into his arms, rolling to the side of the bed and standing with her in his arms. "We'll shower and go eat supper."

"If we shower together, I'll never get supper."

"You're complaining, lady?" he asked with a wicked grin and she had to smile and kiss him.

"No complaints, cowboy," she whispered. "Not the tiniest one."

Two hours later when he turned into the drive to his Pine Valley house, she glanced at him. "What are we doing at your house?"

"I'm going to show you my culinary talents."

"You have—at breakfast, remember?"

"I can do better than oatmeal and toast. How about grilled fillets of bass, caught by my own hands and now cooked by me?"

"You talented rascal, how can I resist you," she teased in a sultry voice, and he grinned.

They sat in his kitchen with a roaring fire in the fireplace, and she ate flaky bites of fish and lemon-covered rice with steamed asparagus. In spite of the delicious food, she was far more fascinated with Aaron, just wanting to watch him, talk to him, be with him. He dug into his pocket and pulled out a small box to set it in front of her.

Curious, she looked at him and then at the box. She opened it and gasped with pleasure as she lifted out a gold link bracelet. "Oh, Aaron, this is beautiful! I love this! Thank you!"

He looked pleased as he fastened it on her wrist, and she came around to give him a kiss. His arm slipped around her waist, but she pulled away from him and sat down again facing him. "We should eat dinner and never let this cooking go to waste."

"Sure, darlin','" he drawled.

He held her hand while they ate as if he couldn't bear to let go of her. After she stopped eating, he set down his glass of water and studied her. While his expression didn't change, she could see that frightening coldness come into his green eyes. "What's wrong, Aaron?"

"Dakota told me about Garth Johannes," Aaron said solemnly. "For a while I get to take you wherever you need to go."

"Aaron, that's ridiculous! The man didn't hurt me. He just said he wanted to ask me more questions, and I told him no."

"Good for you, but damn him. Exactly what did he say to you?"

"I don't remember precisely," she said, looking away, and Aaron turned her to face him.

"You are one poor liar, darlin'. Lack of experience probably causes that. What did he say to you?"

"Drop it, Aaron. It'll just make you angry."

"I'm getting more angry by the minute and imagining the worst. I may go punch him out just because my imagination—"

"Aaron, don't! Please don't do something violent. He just said he hadn't seen me around town much lately. He said it was probably because I was with you. He told me he wanted to ask me a few more questions."

"Dakota said he blocked your way to your car."

"We were on Main Street, for heaven's sake!"

"Don't ever get close enough to him that he can grab you. Promise me."

"Now you're scaring me," she said quietly, looking at the solemn expression on Aaron's face. "I have no intention of getting close to him or his revolting partner."

"Shortly before that—I guess while you were getting your hair cut, I met with him and the other one, Yungst."

"What did you think?" she asked, feeling an intrusion into the warm glow of the evening.

"Probably the same reaction you had. I didn't like them. I don't believe much of anything they said. They know you're expecting and they know the baby is mine."

"How do they know that! I didn't think anyone else knew it yet except Dr. Woodbury and now—" She stopped, remembering seeing the door close at the end of the hall when she had been talking to Aaron in front of the obstetrician's office. "The doctor's office."

"Right. They sort of tipped their own hand by saying that to me. I didn't get much out of them, but I don't trust them or like them. Dakota is watching them. That's why he was there today."

"I wasn't sure Dakota knew who I was, but I've met him before."

"He knows you. He's older than you—like I am," Aaron added dryly.

"You poor decrepit thing," she teased, leaving her dinner and coming around to sit on his lap. "Let me feel and see if you're falling apart," she said, running her hand along his thigh.

He wrapped his arms around her. "This is good, lady. Very good. And I'll show you decrepit," he said, leaning forward to kiss her.

After a few minutes she pushed him away slightly. "Aaron, I interrupted you. You were telling me about Dakota Lewis. What did you start to say?"

"Just that Dakota is trying to watch Johannes and Yungst. Until today, he hasn't seen them do anything they shouldn't.

He said they usually split up, so he can only watch one at a time. They know we're watching them.''

She sobered, thinking about the danger and the missing diamond.

"Stop worrying. We're safely locked away in my house, and no one is watching this place except the security guard. Now I was going to prove that I'm not decrepit and falling apart yet," he said, standing and slinging her over his shoulder.

With a squeal, she laughed as he crossed the room to the oval rug in front of the fireplace. With a flick of the switch, Aaron turned off the lights and only the glow of the fire gave them light.

"Come here, woman," he said, setting her on her feet. He had his feet apart, his legs braced, and he hauled her into his arms, leaning over her. Her laughter vanished with his passionate kiss, and in minutes she was returning kiss for kiss and caress for caress as they loved again long into the night.

As she lay in Aaron's arms with moonlight spilling over them and embers glowing in the fireplace in his large bedroom, he rolled away and crossed the room. She watched him, looking at his lean, muscular, naked body and long legs and her heart pounded with mixed emotions. She knew she had to end their lovemaking or else agree to his proposal. Yet her feelings still hadn't changed.

He picked something up off his desk and sauntered back to bed, sliding beneath the covers beside her to take her into his arms again.

"That was too long away from you."

"That's foolishness, Aaron."

He turned away and she heard a click, and then he settled back with his arms going around her again. He picked up her hand and held out a ring. "Please marry me, Pamela."

Her heart missed a beat. As tears stung her eyes, a knot turned in her throat and hurt overwhelmed her. The diamond was huge, catching moonlight and holding out glittering promises of dreams come true.

She wanted to cry out, *Yes, yes* and throw herself into his arms and stop thinking about tomorrow and the life Aaron had away from Texas and all his background and wealth. But she couldn't shut out his heritage. It was as much a part of him as his Texas upbringing and she still couldn't see herself, a plain elementary teacher from Royal, Texas, holding a lifelong fascination for the sophisticated diplomat that he truly was.

"Aaron…" she said, unable to stop the tears from spilling over. She couldn't talk and all she could do was shake her head. "No. No," she whispered. "I haven't changed how I feel. I don't think this will last. Not for you. You'll have regrets—"

"Dammit, lady, let me make that decision! I'm in love. You're everything I want and have dreamed about—"

"Oh, please, Aaron. That's not true and don't tell me it is. You're infatuated, lost in the fun and the sex we've had, but there's more to life than that. And there's your family. I know how they'll see me."

"They'll see you like I see you, and you're marrying me. They don't get a say in this decision. And it's ridiculous to worry about them because they'll love you when they meet you," he said, sitting up and letting the covers fall around his waist.

She shook her head. "I can't take your ring. I don't feel any differently. I can't resist loving you—you know that," she said, barely able to breathe or say the words and hurting all over. "I can't resist your kisses, but all the loving doesn't change my mind about the future."

He framed her face with his hands, winding his fingers in her hair. "I love you, now and forever."

"Aaron, stop! You're just caught up in the moment." She scrambled away and grabbed a blanket to wrap around herself as she stood. "I have to go home. Now."

She rushed across the room, gathering her clothes, barely aware of what she was doing, moving by rote, knowing this was what she had to do and she had brought this moment on

herself by letting down all the barriers and making love with
him.

She rushed into the bathroom and closed the door, gasping
for breath while tears continued to stream down her face. "I'm
right, Aaron," she whispered. "I know I am. When it's out
that I'm pregnant with your baby, your family won't love me.
Gossip will fly in town, and folks will see me like my mother.
I don't want you involved in my old problems."

With shaking hands she dressed swiftly. When she came
out of the bathroom, he was seated on a chair with his elbows
on his knees. Dressed in jeans and a T-shirt, he raised his head
to look at her. "You're wrong, Mellie."

"I can get home by myself."

"No, you don't," he said, standing. "I'll take you home
and I'm staying when we get there, whether we talk or not.
Lady, you may be in danger—another fact you fail to face."

He took her arm and they went downstairs to his pickup
and rode in an uncomfortable silence to her apartment. She
knew it was useless to protest his staying with her. Thirty
minutes later as she stepped from the bathroom in her robe,
he stood in the hall. He had shed his shirt and wore only his
jeans, and he stood with one hip canted against the wall while
he studied her.

"I know how to be patient. I love you and want to marry
you. And I want to be a father to my baby."

"I have to do what I think is right for you, for me and for
the baby."

"Well, you're blind to the truth. I don't see how you can
think going our separate ways will be good for any of us."

"I think you're the one who's blind to reality," she said
gently, hurting more than she thought was possible. "And I
think we need some distance between us for a while to really
think things through."

"Not while you're in possible danger," he said tersely. A
muscle worked in his jaw and while he looked relaxed, leaning
lightly against the wall, she saw one fist was clenched, his
knuckles white.

"If you were away from me, you might feel differently about all this."

"I was away from you for a month in Spain."

"I don't want to rush into marriage. The minute you found out about the baby, you were in love. Not before, Aaron. That isn't the way it should be." She hurried past him to her room and closed the door, sagging against it, surprised he had let her pass without stopping her.

As she crossed the room, for the first time she noticed the blinking light on her answering machine. She punched the button to hear her messages and received two. The first was from Nancy, her neighbor, to tell her Handley's had left a bouquet for her and Nancy had the roses at her place. Pamela shook her head, thinking about all the dozens of flowers Aaron had sent her, the dazzling ring and life he had offered to her tonight. The next voice came on:

"Pamela, it's Jessica. They have an opening right now in one of the Fort Worth elementary schools. I know the principal—he called me to see if I knew anyone who could fill the position because they're desperate. One of the teachers had to quit in the middle of the semester to take care of her mother. They're going to fill this immediately so you need to talk to them tomorrow if possible. I've tried to get you all evening. Give me a call, no matter how late tonight."

Pamela stared into the darkness. A teaching job in Fort Worth would take her away from Aaron, and she knew it was the right thing to do. Reluctantly, she reached for the phone.

Three hours later, long before dawn, she wrote a note to Aaron. She propped it on the kitchen table and, taking great care to turn off the alarm and not make any noise, she let herself out of the apartment. She suspected she could never have slipped out at his house without waking him, but people came and went all hours of the day and night at her apartment complex and the place was never quiet like his neighborhood. A car starting up wouldn't jolt him out of sleep here.

She looked at his pickup parked next to her car and ran her hand along the door. "Goodbye, Aaron. I love you," she whispered. As she unlocked the door to her car, she glanced around, aware someone could be watching her, but at the moment, caring very little and unable to see for the blur of her tears.

She slid behind the wheel and locked her car doors, driving out of the complex before she needed to switch on her car lights. As she accelerated and headed for the highway, she felt as if her heart was breaking into a million shattered pieces that would never fit back together.

Ten

Aaron came awake, staring into the quiet living room. A faint border of light showed around the edges of the blinds. He stretched and sat up, knowing things weren't right. For the first time, he began to wonder if he would ever get across to Pamela his feelings for her.

Whatever happened, he intended to be at her side for the birth of their baby. In frustration he ran his fingers through his hair. For once in his life, words had failed him, and he had been unable to convince her about his feelings. Marriage to her was the most important thing in his life. She didn't believe he knew his own feelings. And she couldn't stop seeing herself as too country for him.

He loved the woman with all his heart. He was as sure of that as he was certain he was a Texan. Why couldn't she see it? He had tried every way he knew how to show her.

"Darlin', you're a stubborn woman," he said softly, shaking his head. He didn't want to put any distance between them. Far from it. He wanted her in his arms and in his bed every night of his life. Life was empty and cold without her. He rubbed his neck, kinked from sleeping on her short sofa. His whole life was in a kink over this woman.

He stood and stretched, yanking on briefs and jeans. He didn't want to wake her, and went to the kitchen to start breakfast, trying to be quiet as he poured orange juice and fixed himself a piece of toast. He went back to the living room to fold up his covers. He tiptoed out the front door to get the Royal newspaper and the Dallas newspaper and then he sat in the kitchen, reading. When he was through with both papers, he moved restlessly. She was never this late getting up. He glanced at his watch. Almost eight in the morning. He had appointments and needed to shower and shave.

He turned and looked at the alarm and saw it was turned off. He crossed the room to look at it closely and then started to go to her room when he noticed a note propped on the counter with his name scrawled across the front of the folded paper. How had he missed seeing this earlier?

Cold dread enveloped him as he crossed the narrow space and picked up the note. Knowing what he would find, he didn't want to read it.

Dear Aaron:

I think we need some time and distance to sort feelings out. I have friends, I have a job and I'll be very careful. Take care of yourself.

Love, Pamela.

He let the note flutter from his hands to the counter as he walked to the window and opened the blinds. Her car was gone and only his pickup was in the carport.

Where had she gone? How long since she'd left? How long had she planned leaving him? She already had a job and hadn't told him?

He hurt with a consuming pain that immobilized him. "Dammit," he swore, worrying about her safety. He whirled around and hurried to the bathroom to dress and start searching for her.

As he drove to his Pine Valley home, he called Dakota on his cellular phone.

"Dakota, Pamela's gone and she didn't leave word where she was going. She wants to be on her own for a while, but I'm worried about her. Keep those two under surveillance as much as you can, will you?"

"Sure. I'll get a friend to help. Anything else I can do?"

"If there is, I'll let you know. Thanks."

Aaron punched off the phone. "Dammit, Mellie. This isn't the time to slip off without letting anyone know where you are or what you're doing." He prayed she hadn't been followed from her apartment and tried to reassure himself with the fact that he hadn't seen anyone following them for several days now. But if someone discovered she had gone off alone…

"Dammit," he swore again, pressing the accelerator and feeling a sense of urgency to find her as quickly as possible, not only for himself, but for her safety.

"She doesn't want you to find her," he reminded himself and grimaced. If she wanted to get off by herself to think things over, he didn't want to crowd her, but he was worried about her. And he thought they had been so close to an end to all her foolish notions that she wasn't the woman for him. Couldn't the lady see that she was the *only* woman for him?

By noon Aaron felt as if the earth had opened up and swallowed her. He couldn't find a trace of her from her neighbors, and he had to wait until school was out to talk to her teacher friends. Shortly before school was out, he went to see the principal of the school where she had taught, remembering Thad Delner from the Texas Cattleman's Club gala the night he met Pamela.

Within minutes after sitting in Thad Delner's office, Aaron's frustrations increased. The principal sat behind his desk and studied Aaron. "I remember you from the gala. I think you took her home that night, and I hear you've been dating lately."

"Yes, sir, we have. I've asked Pamela to marry me."

"Ah, congratulations. Pamela is an excellent teacher, a wonderful person."

"I think so. Right now, I'd like to find her because I'm worried about her safety. I've been staying with her or she's stayed at my place since someone broke into her apartment and trashed it. She left a note that she was going to see a friend, but I'm concerned for her safety."

"Have you talked to the police?"

"Not yet. I thought if I can find out where she is, I can talk to her myself."

"I'm sorry, Mr. Black. I can't help you. I don't know all of her friends. My teachers' lives are their own, for the most part, once they leave my school."

Feeling restless and knowing he was at a dead end here, Aaron stood and offered his hand. "Thanks. If you don't mind, as soon as school is out, I'd like to talk to several of the teachers who are her close friends."

"That's fine. In about five minutes the bell should ring. If you'd like, you're welcome to wait here in the office until school is dismissed."

"Thanks, I'll be fine."

As soon as the building emptied of students, Aaron talked to three teachers before he found a woman named Sally Grayson who told him Pamela's best friend was Jessica Atkins who lived in Midland.

Within the hour Aaron was in his pickup driving to Midland. He had already learned Jessica had an unlisted phone number, but with the help of Dakota Lewis, he had found Jessica's address.

In Fort Worth, Pamela left the principal's office and stepped into the sunshine. It had been a little over twelve hours since she'd left Aaron at her apartment. Not long enough for any of the pain to dull. Now she had a job in Fort Worth and would start Monday morning teaching second grade. It was what she wanted and what she thought she should do, but why did it seem so wrong? She hurt constantly and could barely carry on a coherent conversation. She suspected she would never have gotten the job except that the school was desperate and she had come highly recommended, but during her interview, she'd had difficulty concentrating on anything the principal had said to her.

She hurried to her car parked in visitor parking and looked back at the school. Only three years old and made of brick and glass, the sprawling elementary school had state-of-the-art equipment, and her salary would be an increase over what she had made in Royal, yet she didn't feel anything except a deep sense of resignation for doing what she had to do.

The morning sickness was as bad as ever, and she prayed she could handle her nausea. Wind caught her hair, blowing it across her cheek. Next she had a list of apartments to look at. The sooner she made the move, the better off she would be. She suspected Aaron would not give up easily, and when he found her, she wanted to be in her own apartment, working at her new job. In order to give her a little time to get settled, she had wrung a promise out of Jessica not to tell Aaron where she had gone.

Time to get settled and to heal. She wondered if she would ever heal over the hurt of telling him goodbye. And why was it nagging at her that she was making a mistake? She had been over and over it, but everything had been so good between them and the tempting thought of letting go of her doubts and marrying him, giving their baby a father, tore at her.

She straightened her shoulders. "Remember his background, his life away from Royal. Get real, woman. You're country and he is not. Maybe a bit of cowboy still lingers in him, but he is so much else."

She looked at her map of the area and at the list of apartments, hoping she could find something close to the school. Suddenly she was swamped with loss, missing Aaron, knowing what she was losing, and she had to lean her head against the steering wheel while she cried. It hurt so badly because she missed him dreadfully.

She spent the rest of the day looking at apartments, none of which appealed to her, and early in the evening went back to her motel room on the Midland highway. She drove slowly and carefully, knowing that her full attention wasn't on her driving.

That night she could eat only a few bites of dinner and cried herself to sleep, missing Aaron more with each passing minute. While she kept telling herself the pain would dull with time and finally heal, the loss hurt badly, and she couldn't believe her own words.

The next morning she spent the first hours nauseated and crying. With determination, she left the motel, a list of available apartments in hand to begin another day's search for a place to live.

Late in the afternoon she made a deposit on a small, one-bedroom apartment that was sunny, filled with windows. She hoped it would be cheerful to come home to, but as she stood signing papers, she could only think how empty it looked and remember Aaron sprawled on her short sofa, his long legs dangling off. She missed him every second of the day. Missed him to distraction.

"You need to sign here, Miss Miles."

"I'm sorry," Pamela said, coming out of her daze and staring at her new blond landlady. She couldn't even remember the woman's name. Pamela took the pen and signed her name, handing over her check for the deposit.

"It's a very quiet place, and you'll have a swimming pool and clubhouse facilities."

"That's nice. Thank you," Pamela said, barely hearing the woman. She accepted a key, glancing once more at the place that would be her new home. A home for her and their baby. *Aaron's baby.*

As tears welled in her eyes, she was aware her landlady was staring at her. "Thank you," she mumbled, accepting the key and turning away before she was crying uncontrollably.

As soon as she was in her car, she jotted down the address again, certain she wouldn't remember it an hour from now. She went out to eat, barely able to get anything down, knowing the hardest part was ahead of her because she had to go back to Royal and get her things and move. And she would see Aaron.

It was dusk when she left the restaurant and drove back to the motel. She was exhausted, still hurting as much as ever. She turned the corner to her room and gripped the steering wheel in a moment of déjà vu when she looked at the shiny black pickup parked in front of her motel door.

Aaron watched her drive up, and his heart was in his throat. He had rehearsed what he would say to her, but his practiced arguments were forgotten when she stepped out of her car and stood facing him. All color drained from her face. She looked haggard, her eyes red, yet she still was the most beautiful woman on earth to him.

For the first time in his life, he had nothing to say. He felt helpless and adrift, wanting with all his heart and soul to let her know the depth of his feelings for her. He walked over to her and took her into his arms.

Pamela looked up at the tall man holding her, and fought her tears and tried to conjure up the words she knew she should say, but then he leaned down. His mouth covered hers, and words were gone while he kissed her as if he had waited years for this kiss.

"Mellie," he whispered. Shocked, Pamela tasted salty tears and leaned back to look at him, stunned that this tough, worldly cowboy diplomat was shedding tears. She looked into his green eyes and saw that he was as torn with hurt as she. It was astonishing. Impossible. A moment of revelation. Aaron, hurting enough to *cry* over her?

"You love me," she whispered.

"I've been trying to convince you of my love for the past month," he said roughly, swiping at his face. "You're my life, woman. I'm not fit for anything without you. I love you, Mellie.''

"Oh, Aaron," she said in awe, letting go of her doubts and fears and wrapping her arms tightly around his neck as she stood on tiptoe to kiss him. "I love you. I missed you." She leaned back. "You're sure? I don't know anything about fancy balls and the life you lead overseas."

"You can learn it just like I did. You think I knew about it when I left Royal? And if you really don't want that, we can stay home. I can live on the ranch. I'm as good a cowpoke as a diplomat."

"You'd give up your diplomatic career if I wanted you to?" she asked, beginning to realize the depth of his love and feeling as if boulders were lifting off her heart. "Oh, Aaron!" She threw herself against him to kiss him.

His arms banded her tightly as he leaned down to kiss her long and hungrily. He raised his head, dug in his pocket and pulled out the engagement ring. "Will you marry me?"

"Yes! Oh, yes, yes, yes!"

He kissed her again, longer this time, and then raised his head to look down at her. "We'll have a big fancy church wedding with family and friends."

"I don't have to, Aaron."

"I know you don't, but I want one. My family will love an excuse to get together."

"Your family! Aaron, they're not going to—"

"Yes, they're going to love you like I do. You'll see. What do you think I have for a family—a bunch of cold-hearted monsters?"

"Of course not."

"They're lovable like me. Now what we're going to do— we'll have that wedding and it will all be official and a big deal, but for tonight, I don't want to wait. You said yes and I don't want any cold feet or worries. I want to find a justice of the peace and get married right now."

"Get married twice?" she said, laughing and feeling giddy.

"Yes, darlin'," he drawled. "I'm not letting you get out of my sight until you're Mrs. Aaron Black."

"Mrs. Aaron Black," she repeated, unable to believe it and touching his cheek, feeling the rough stubble.

"I didn't shave. I had to wring where you were out of your friend."

"She promised me she wouldn't tell you, and Jessica has never gone back on a promise."

His eyes twinkled. "I did a little sweet-talking and she saw things my way."

"Aaron, you're impossible."

"C'mon. We're wasting time here."

She couldn't stop touching him any more than he could keep his hands from her while they found a justice of the peace and were married with two neighbors as witnesses. By nine o'clock they were in the bridal suite of a hotel in Fort Worth, a room with a balcony and a view of the lights of the city sprawled below, but she had eyes only for Aaron as she stepped into his arms.

"I'm not dressed for a wedding."

"It doesn't matter. You'll be undressed in minutes," he whispered as he pulled her into his arms to kiss her hungrily. "I want you with me the rest of my life, darlin'," he said, showering kisses on her throat as he twisted free the buttons of her blue shirt and pushed it away from her shoulders.

Suddenly she leaned away from him. "Aaron! I forgot! I have a job and an apartment I leased for the next six months. I have to be at work Monday morning."

"No, you don't."

"I signed a contract for the apartment, and I have a verbal contract for the job."

"Darlin', my big brother is ever so good at untangling things like contracts and commitments. We'll turn the problem of your new job and apartment over to him and he'll get you out of the deals and he'll find someone else to teach in your place." Aaron unfastened her bra and cupped her breast. "Don't give it another thought," he said in a husky voice.

She closed her eyes and moaned, the worries already vanished as she tugged at his belt. "You and these big Texas belt buckles."

"It's easy. A flick of the wrist," he whispered unfastening his belt and bending down to stroke her nipple with his tongue.

"Oh, Aaron, I love you, love you."

He framed her face with his hands, looking into her eyes. "I love you, Mellie, with all my being. Mrs. Aaron Black, my wife, my love." He wrapped his arms around her to kiss her, and she melted into his embrace, sliding his shirt off his shoulders and running her hands across his bare back.

He picked her up to carry her to bed and she clung to him, happiness filling her and a sense of everything being right once again in her world.

Epilogue

Pamela hurried across the foyer of the church.

Looking handsome in his black tux, Matt Walker stood waiting. His expression was solemn and preoccupied, but as he took her arm, he smiled down at her. "You look gorgeous."

"Thank you. Matt, I can't tell you how much I appreciate your standing in for the father I never had. The minute this service is over, you go on back to the hospital. You don't have to come out to the ranch for the reception."

"I'm going to take you up on that, Pam. Dusty Winthrop, one of my best hands, is standing watch for me."

"Miss Miles, Mr. Walker." The wedding coordinator peered at them over her glasses. "It's time." She hurried around to straighten out the train of Pamela's wedding dress.

As they began to move toward the center aisle, Pamela looked up at Matt. "You're the most handsome man any bride ever had escort her down an aisle."

Matt grinned. "Aaron can't stop grinning and he can't carry on a coherent conversation, so we need to get this over with."

As she smiled, her gaze ran over the crowd that stood and turned to face them. She couldn't believe this was happening to her. Aaron had paid for everything and heaven knows what it had cost him to pull this all together within days. Jessica was her maid of honor, and after she'd met Rebecca, Aaron's sister, Pamela had asked Rebecca to be a bridesmaid. Aaron had been right. All his family were friendly and welcoming and she knew she was going to be good friends with Rebecca who had accompanied her to the church today. When they'd arrived, the two had been alone for a few minutes.

Rebecca had hung up the wedding dress, helping Pamela with her things in the dressing room. "My brother looks like he's going to explode with happiness." She turned to face Pamela. "I'm so glad you're marrying him and you'll be my sister-in-law. I didn't know my brother had such great taste, finding someone like you."

"Thanks, Rebecca. I'm so in love with him and now I'm falling in love with his family. I only had my mother and there were always problems."

"That's over. Forget it," Rebecca said with a dismissive wave of her hand.

"Rebecca, we haven't told anyone—well, I've told Jessica, but no one else—we're going to have a baby. I'm pregnant."

Rebecca's mouth opened and her eyes widened and then she flew across the room to hug Pamela who let out her breath. Now she knew everything would be all right with his sister.

"I'm thrilled. Oh, have a girl. We need more girls in this family. I'm so happy for both of you. And I'll keep your secret. Don't worry," she said, her eyes twinkling.

The door opened and Jessica entered and the conversation changed, but Pamela felt as if another weight had lifted off her heart.

As she walked down the aisle, she looked at Aaron and joy warmed her heart. Her Aaron, the love of her life. He looked breathtakingly handsome in his black tux, but then she looked

into his green eyes and forgot the wedding, the crowd, everything except the man waiting to marry her for the second time.

As Matt placed her hand in Aaron's, she looked up at him
and couldn't wait to be alone with him again.

His brother officiated, and his other brother, Jeb, was best
man. As she looked at Jacob Black, she could see little resem-
blance in the two brothers. The Reverend Jacob Black was
stocky, blue-eyed and only their brown hair was similar. Aaron
and his brother, Jeb, looked far more alike with their height,
green eyes, brown hair and lean builds.

With Aaron, she repeated wedding vows, and Aaron slipped
a gold band onto her finger. After a blessing and prayer, Reverend Black declared them husband and wife.

Aaron raised her veil and leaned down to kiss her. She
placed her hand on his shoulder and kissed him briefly. He
raised his head. "Race you up the aisle."

She laughed as he turned, stretched out his legs and gave
Matt a high-five when he passed him. She tried to keep up
with Aaron's long stride.

"You weren't joking."

"I want you alone in bed with me, darlin'. We're not staying long at the ranch, and my family knows that. Our guests
can party until tomorrow, but I have other plans for you. We'll
have our own party, darlin'."

"Your sister and brothers—"

"I had my visit with them during the past few days."

They raced to a limo and the driver pulled away, speeding
out of Royal to the Black ranch and from the moment they
settled in the back seat, Aaron closed them off from the view
of the driver and pulled her into his arms to kiss her.

An hour later on the lawn behind the ranch house, Pamela
stood talking to Jessica who moved away to get a piece of
cake. Within moments Rebecca sauntered up. "I've told
Aaron goodbye and will tell you goodbye now. My flight
leaves this evening."

"I'm so glad you were here," Pamela said, meaning it
wholeheartedly.

"You'll see more of me. I'm thinking of coming home and opening a practice here."

"For selfish reasons, I'm glad, but we'll be in Spain."

"He'll come home eventually. You can't keep Aaron away from Texas."

Pamela looked across the lawn as a breeze tugged at her hair. She saw her handsome husband standing with a cluster of his Texas Cattleman's Club friends and wondered if they were talking horses, football or the missing diamond. For a time, she would be glad to leave the danger and problems behind, but she knew they were having a short honeymoon because Aaron wanted to get back to Royal to help his friends. When he turned his head, his gaze met hers and she felt as if he had reached out and touched her.

Aaron turned back to his friends, looking at Dakota, Ben, Justin and Greg Hunt who had joined them as well as the fellow Cattleman members Forrest Cunningham and Hank Langley. Greg, Forrest and Hank were interested in the problems the other club members were facing.

"Matt went back to the hospital to watch Lady Helena,"

"That red diamond has to be here in Royal," Dakota said.

"Pamela and I won't be gone long and then I'll be back in Royal. Dakota, you and Matt both have my pager number and my cell phone number if you need to reach me."

"Yeah, I'm sure you'll answer your cell phone on your honeymoon."

Aaron grinned and looked across the lawn at Pamela who took his breath every time he glanced at her. In a white satin and lace wedding dress, she looked regal and beautiful, but he wanted her alone and naked in his arms.

He heard his friends discussing the burned scrap of paper found at the landing site, speculating on the little they could read, but he barely listened.

"The coroner agreed to see me Monday," Dakota said, "and Sheriff Escobar has agreed. Maybe we can learn a little more about Riley Monroe's death. Ben, are you still watching Jamie?"

"Yes, I am. Not a difficult task, and I am going to say goodbye now because I do not want her out of my sight." He looked at Aaron and offered his hand. "May all happiness come to you and your beautiful bride," he said.

"Thanks, Ben," Aaron said, shaking his hand and watching his friend stride away, the long robe swishing around his legs. Aaron moved impatiently. "Excuse me, my friends, I'm getting my bride and getting the hell out of here."

They laughed and gave him congratulations and best wishes as he walked away. He told his brothers goodbye and then found Pamela, slipping his arm through hers. "I need to see you," he said, smiling at the group of friends clustered around her before he whisked her away.

"C'mon. I have a car waiting and we're going."

They rushed through the house and to the long, four-car garage. Aaron held open the door to a two-door black sports car that she had never ridden in before, and in minutes they were roaring away from the house, stirring up a plume of dust on the lane that led to the highway.

As he drove, Aaron tugged off his tie and then thrust out his hand. "Get the links out of my cuffs?"

"I think you should keep both hands on the wheel and pay attention to your driving. Do you know how fast you're going?"

"Do you know how badly I want to be alone with you and not have to concentrate on anything except you?"

She smiled as she tugged free his gold cuff link. She held his wrist and raised it to trail kisses across his knuckles.

"Maybe we'll just pull off in the bushes and I'll have my way with you right here," he said in a husky, threatening voice, and she laughed.

"Behind a mesquite in a bed of cactus? I don't think so, Aaron. You put both hands on the wheel and drive."

On the Black private jet he held her on his lap and kissed her until she pushed against him. "I'm going to change out of this wedding dress."

"Let me help."

"No! I'll be right back." She slid off his lap and he stood and retrieved a bag for her, handing it to her while his gaze devoured her.

With excitement bubbling in her, she hurried to change to a simple black sheath that buttoned down the back. The moment she returned, Aaron pulled her back onto his lap and kissed her, his hands sliding over her until she caught his wrists.

"You wait to go any farther until we're alone!"

"Monty is flying the plane. He's not paying any attention to us."

"I don't care. Behave, Aaron." She gazed into his eyes that held such scalding desire that her pulse raced.

"I need to talk to you," Aaron said while his fingers played in her hair. "I finally got my boss in D.C."

"And?" she asked, unable to tell from Aaron's expression whether he was going to relate good news or bad.

"I told them we wanted our baby to be born in Texas."

"You did!" she exclaimed, surprised because she had expected to move back to Spain right away.

"I want our baby born in Texas. Not anywhere else. So we're here until the baby comes. Then, they've offered me a position as an ambassador to a tiny, obscure country in Europe, San Raimundo."

"Aaron, no matter how small the country, that's an incredible promotion for you, isn't it?"

"Yes, it is," he replied solemnly. "What about it? Do you want me to take it or not?"

She was astounded he was asking. He seemed so forceful, so determined in everything he did and she knew this was an undreamed of promotion. "Oh, Aaron, of course, you'll take it." Tears welled up and she kissed him, feeling his arms tighten around her.

When she pushed away to look at him, she had her emotions under control. "Congratulations on your promotion. That's fantastic."

"Thanks. There's more. I thought you'd agree, so I told

them I'd take the ambassadorship, but I will retire in six or seven years because our baby needs to go to school here.''

"You went to school in England. They have marvelous schools.''

"You don't want to come home to Texas?''

"Of course I do!'' she said, suspecting that in six or seven years, she would want to be living in Texas.

"We'll come home and settle on the ranch if that's all right.''

"You have this all mapped out, don't you?'' she asked, realizing he had her life planned.

"Sort of. What about ranch life? You're a town gal. Think you can take the ranch?''

"Of course I can. You'll be there and I'll love it.''

"Good.'' He gazed out the window of the jet at the deep blue sky. "Someday I may go into politics and we'll be back in Washington, but we'll worry about that when the time comes.''

"In all your planning, you better schedule in a little brother or sister for this baby, Aaron.''

His gaze swung back to her, and he stroked her cheek. "I haven't ever asked you—how many children do you want?''

"I would like five. That's adding to overpopulation, but they'll be brilliant like their father and a real asset to the world. And you can afford five, Aaron.''

"That I can. Five sounds grand to me.'' His expression became more solemn. "The Texas Cattleman's Club guys want my help, too. That's another reason not to rush back to Spain right away. We need to find that missing diamond because until we do, I think there is a lot of danger in Royal. Now, my lovely bride, it's been far too long since we kissed.''

It was an hour before Aaron locked the hotel door and turned to her. Her heart thudded with eager anticipation and she ran into his arms, winding her arms around his neck and pulling his head down to kiss him. He had already shed his tux coat and now studs flew and his shirt was gone. Locks of brown hair fell over his forehead and his green eyes held fires that scalded her. "Turn around and let me get you out of that dress," he said.

When she turned, she felt his hands lock in the neckline of her dress as he trailed his tongue across her nape and started wild tingles coursing in her.

"Aaron, no!" she said, whirling out of his grasp. "You unfasten the buttons. I'm keeping this dress, too, for memories of today."

"I can get it sewed up."

"No! Promise me—"

"We're wasting time. Turn around. I'll unbutton—what, three hundred buttons—damnation!"

She laughed softly and turned her back to him. "Don't be absurd! More like twenty buttons, but you started this, so you finish it carefully."

"Sure, darlin'," he said, kissing her nape and trailing kisses lower over her back as he unfastened her dress. He tossed it on the bed and picked her up to sit down on the bed and hold her in his lap. She wore a white satin-and-lace teddy while he had on his black tux pants. As she ran her hand across his chest, his arms tightened around her.

"My love," he whispered before he kissed her. "Mrs. Aaron Black."

"Being married is wonderful, and I'll never get tired of being called Mrs. Black. I love you, Aaron, with my whole heart."

"I love you with all my heart and soul." He lowered his head to kiss her. She clung to him and returned his kisses, her heart thudding with joy. Mrs. Aaron Black. How wonderful life was! Happiness filled her along with joy for her tall, lean husband. She knew he truly did love her. "Oh, Aaron! You're my life, my family, my all."

He leaned over her to kiss her again, and she tightened her arms around him, eagerly winding her fingers in his hair and knowing her love for him would last the rest of their lives.

Aaron shifted slightly to look at her, his green eyes filled with warmth. "I'm going to spend our forever showing you how much I love you, darlin'."

"I'm trusting you will," she said, as she pulled him closer to kiss him.

*   *   *   *   *

Watch for the next installment of the

TEXAS CATTLEMAN'S CLUB: LONE STAR JEWELS

*where a royally Texan romance
is played out between
Lady Helena Reichard and
cattle baron Matt Walker,
and more of the ultrasecret mission
to uncover the missing jewel
is revealed in*

LONE STAR KNIGHT

*by Cindy Gerard
Coming to you from Silhouette Desire in
March 2001.*

*And now for a sneak preview of
LONE STAR KNIGHT,
please turn the page.*

One

It wasn't true. Not completely. Your entire life didn't flash before you when you were about to die. Only bits and pieces, old, unrelated little snippets scrolled by like a vivid Technicolor collage—along with an extreme and acute awareness of those who were about to die with you.

While the flight crew and eleven other men and women in the charter jet bound from Royal, Texas, to the European principality of Asterland prepared for the crash landing with stalwart optimism, whispered prayers, or soft weeping, Lady Helena Reichard thought silently of Asterland, the home she might never see again. She thought of her parents, the Earl and Countess of Orion, and the pain her death would cause them.

Oddly, she thought of the tall, handsome Texan with smiling green eyes and dark curling hair who had waltzed her round the dance floor at the Texas Cattleman's Club reception just two nights past.

She'd met commanding men before. Sophisticated.

Worldly. Titled and moneyed. She hadn't, however, met anyone like Matthew Walker. With his quick, slashing smile and
devastating wit, he'd been at once charming yet subtly and
purposefully aloof. He was obviously a man of wealth, yet the
hand that had held hers in its strong grip had worn the calluses
of physical labor without apology. His polished and gallant
formality had been a fascinating foil for an understated man-
of-the-earth essence that had both intrigued and captivated—
and left her wishing she hadn't had to leave Royal, Texas, so
soon.

How sad, she thought, that she'd been denied the chance to
know him better. How sad that her last glimpse of Texas
would be from five hundred feet and falling. And then she
thought of nothing but the moment as the jet, its left engine
shooting fire, lurched, shuddered and dropped the last one hundred feet to the ground. She lowered her head, wrapped her
arms around her ankles and prepared for impact....

Matt Walker was striding wearily toward the burn unit
nurses' station when he spotted Dr. Justin Webb, dressed in
green scrubs, heading for the elevator. "Hey, Justin, wait up."

Justin turned and scowled at Matt. "I've done admits on
patients who look better than you."

Matt knew exactly what his friend saw: five o'clock
shadow, badly rumpled shirt and bloodshot eyes. He scrubbed
a hand over his unshaven jaw, rolled the stiffness out of his
shoulders. "I'm fine. Just a long night."

Justin snorted. "More like a lot of long nights."

It had been almost two months since the plane crash landing
that had resulted in Lady Helena Reichard's emergency ad-
mission to the burn unit at Royal Memorial Hospital. She had
been among a group of Asterland dignitaries and a few lo-
cals—Matt's friends Pamela Black and Jamie Morris among
them—who were en route to Asterland after a posh diplomatic
reception at the club. Close to a full month had passed since
Matt had been assigned by his fellow Texas Cattleman's Club
members to stand guard outside Helena's door.

It didn't much matter that he was beat. His welfare wasn't at stake here. Helena's was. He just wished he knew who, or what, he was protecting her from.

Besides Matt and Justin, only three other club members knew the mysterious details surrounding the charter jet's emergency landing that had sent Helena to the hospital. Though luckily no one was killed, even now, two months later, it was still tough to absorb. The crash had been bad enough. But there'd also been a murder. A jewel theft. The hint of an attempted political coup involving the European Principality of Asterland.

Helena Reichard, it seemed, was stuck smack in the middle of it all; Matt understood exactly how vulnerable she was. He also understood that nothing, absolutely nothing more was going to happen to her under his watch.

"How's she doing?" he asked Justin.

After a glance toward the charge nurse who was busy on the phone, Justin steered Matt toward the sofa at the end of the hall on the pretense of privacy. Matt suspected what Justin really wanted was to get him off his feet. Too tired to make an issue of it, he sat.

"As you already know, most of her burns are second-degree and restricted to her left arm and upper leg." Justin eased down beside him. "It's that nasty patch of third-degree on the back of her left hand that's giving her trouble. We had to graft. Unfortunately, the site's been problematic."

Matt slumped back, rubbed an index finger over his brow. "Infection, right?"

Justin nodded. "It's cleared up now but it set her recovery back. Only time will tell what kind of mobility she'll regain."

Matt thought of the lovely hand he'd held in his at the Cattleman's Club reception and dance. The petal-soft skin. The slim, graceful fingers. "And her ankle?"

Justin shook his head. "That's still up for grabs, too. It's a bad fracture. Even with the surgery and the pins in place, we can't guarantee that she won't have a permanent limp."

Matt stared past Justin's shoulder to the partially open door of Helena's room. He thought of the beautiful, vivacious woman he'd waltzed around the dance floor. The woman whose cornflower-blue eyes had smiled into his with unguarded interest. The woman who had said his name in her perfect, practiced English yet made it sound exotic and made him feel extraordinary. That woman had been beyond perfection.

He didn't have to be inside her head to understand that the woman in the hospital room, though still beautiful, was now badly scarred, potentially disabled—and that here would be much more to her recovery process than knitting bones and healing flesh. And he couldn't throw off the helpless notion that there wasn't a damn thing he could do to help her.

After a long look at Matt, Justin rose. "Look, I can cover for you for a few hours."

"Thanks, but she's *my* assignment, not yours."

Justin's long, measuring look asked the same question Matt had been asking himself lately. *Are you sure this is just an assignment?*

Matt wasn't sure of anything except that he wasn't ready to admit, even to himself yet, that it might be more.

where love comes alive—online...

eHARLEQUIN.com

shop eHarlequin

- ♥ Find all the new Silhouette releases at everyday great discounts.

- ♥ Try before you buy! Read an excerpt from the latest Silhouette novels.

- ♥ Write an online review and share your thoughts with others.

reading room

- ♥ Read our Internet exclusive daily and weekly online serials, or vote in our interactive novel.

- ♥ Talk to other readers about your favorite novels in our Reading Groups.

- ♥ Take our Choose-a-Book quiz to find the series that matches you!

authors' alcove

- ♥ Find out interesting tidbits and details about your favorite authors' lives, interests and writing habits.

- ♥ Ever dreamed of being an author? Enter our Writing Round Robin. The Winning Chapter will be published online! Or review our writing guidelines for submitting your novel.

where love comes alive—online...

eHARLEQUIN.com

your romantic
books

- ♥ Shop online! Visit Shop eHarlequin and discover a wide selection of new releases and classic favorites at great discounted prices.

- ♥ Read our daily and weekly Internet exclusive serials, and participate in our interactive novel in the reading room.

- ♥ Ever dreamed of being a writer? Enter your chapter for a chance to become a featured author in our Writing Round Robin novel.

• • • • • •

your romantic
life

- ♥ Check out our feature articles on dating, flirting and other important romance topics and get your daily love dose with tips on how to keep the romance alive every day.

• • • • • •

your
community

- ♥ Have a Heart-to-Heart with other members about the latest books and meet your favorite authors.

- ♥ Discuss your romantic dilemma in the Tales from the Heart message board.

your romantic
escapes

- ♥ Learn what the stars have in store for you with our daily Passionscopes and weekly Erotiscopes.

- ♥ Get the latest scoop on your favorite royals in Royal Romance.